IN THE TRENCHES

IN THE TRENCHES

A Russian Woman Soldier's Story of World War I

TATIANA L. DUBINSKAYA

EDITED BY LAWRENCE M. KAPLAN

POTOMAC BOOKS | *An imprint of the University of Nebraska Press*

In the Trenches first appeared in Russian as *V okopakh* in 1930. *Machine Gunner* first appeared in Russian as *Pulemetchik* in 1963.

Library of Congress Cataloging-in-Publication Data
Names: Dubinskaia, Tat͡iana Leonidovna, 1902–1990, author. | Kaplan, Lawrence M. (Lawrence Martin), 1954– editor.
Title: In the trenches: a Russian woman soldier's story of World War I / Tatiana L. Dubinskaya; edited by Lawrence M. Kaplan.
Other titles: V okopakh. English
Description: [Lincoln]: Potomac Books, an imprint of the University of Nebraska Press, [2020] | Includes index.
Identifiers: LCCN 2019035104
ISBN 9781640121966 (paperback)
ISBN 9781640123403 (epub)
ISBN 9781640123410 (mobi)
ISBN 9781640123427 (pdf)
Subjects: LCSH: Dubinskaia, Tat͡iana Leonidovna, 1902–1990—Fiction. | World War, 1914–1918—Russia—Participation, Female—Fiction. | Women soldiers—Russia—Fiction. | Kazan' (Russia)—Fiction. | GSAFD: Autobiographical fiction.
Classification: LCC PG3476.D788 V6513 2020 |
DDC 891.73/42—dc23
LC record available at https://lccn.loc.gov/2019035104

Set in Lyon Text by Mikala R. Kolander.

INTRODUCTION

Lawrence M. Kaplan

The Amazons of Greek mythology, a nation of women warriors in Asia, established a historical basis for women as warriors. Prior to the nineteenth century, however, women did not play a large role participating in warfare. There were a few women, such as Queen Boadicea, who led a British tribal revolt against the Romans in the first century AD, and Joan of Arc, a fifteenth-century French patriot who took up arms against the British, but such women were exceptional cases.

It was more common for women disguised as men to participate in direct combat, such as Deborah Sampson in the American Revolution, Esther Manuel in the Napoleonic Wars, and Annie Lillybridge in the American Civil War. In 1782 during the American Revolution, seventeen-year-old Deborah Sampson enlisted in a Massachusetts regiment using an assumed male name and served in the ranks until her sex was discovered the following year at a hospital where she was treated for ill health. After her recovery, she received an honorable discharge, and Congress subsequently awarded her a pension.[1] During the Napoleonic Wars, Esther Manuel, a German mother of two, sought to find her husband fighting in France and assumed a male name to join the army in 1813, where she was twice wounded, rose to the rank of a sergeant-major, and received the Iron Cross, Germany's highest award for valor.[2] During the American Civil War, Annie Lillybridge, a sixteen-year-old girl, fell in love with a lieutenant from a Michigan infantry regiment in the spring of 1862 and wanted to be near him.

She disguised herself as a male, enlisted in another company of his regiment, without his knowledge, and served in the ranks until a shot in the arm disabled her later that year. The army discharged her after several months of hospitalization, while she successfully retained her male disguise.[3]

By the 1850s the role of women in warfare, serving as women, began to expand for nurses and those seeking to participate in civil uprisings. Thanks to Florence Nightingale's pioneering work in nursing during the Crimean War in the mid-1850s, that profession soon opened to women. In the United States, for example, Dorothea Dix used women contract nurses and volunteers as the Superintendent of Women Nurses for the U.S. Army to help care for soldiers during the Civil War (1861–65). The U.S. Army again used women contract nurses during the Spanish-American War (1898), under the supervision of Dr. Anita Newcomb McGee. Following the war the U.S. Army established the Army Nurse Corps (1901) with Dr. McGee as its first director. The Army Nurse Corps continues to hold the distinction of being the oldest military women's organization in the Department of Defense, even though it is no longer exclusively composed of women.

In addition to nursing, collective groups of women began participating in various civil uprisings, beginning in the 1850s. Thousands of Chinese women formed into brigades that fought during the Taiping Rebellion in the early 1850s, a women's battalion participated in the 1871 insurrection of Paris against the French government, and about five hundred Chinese women participated in some military operations and fighting during the 1911 Republican Revolution that toppled the Manchu dynasty.[4]

After World War I began in 1914, there was an influx of women in nursing, clerical, and support roles in the major armies to relieve men for fighting. Some women also continued to take up arms as they had in the past. Nowhere was this more prevalent than in Russia.

Women gained greater acceptance on the battlefield, particularly in Russia. When the war began, the Russian army had a permissive attitude toward women serving in the ranks. Grand Duke Nicholas, the head of the army, reportedly allowed some women to serve in the transport and commissary services, provided they keep away from the firing line. As they saw the men fall in battle, however, some of these women rushed forward to fill the gaps. They participated in direct combat, and afterward local commanders allowed them to keep their positions. Other women took the places of reservist relatives called up who could not serve due to sickness, absence, or other reasons. Their wives or sisters, disguised as males, often took their places and were allowed to remain in the ranks even after their sex was discovered. A few other women, such as Maria Botchkareva, who enlisted as an infantry soldier and later organized the Russian Women's Battalion of Death, and Olga Ellviser, who rejoined the same Cossack regiment she had served with in the Russo-Japanese War (1904–5), received special permission from the army to serve in the ranks as women.[5]

The exploits of women soldiers in the Russian army, typically girl-friends and wives of soldiers, soon began receiving press coverage. For example, in November 1914, the Petrograd correspondent of Great Britain's *Morning Post* reported: "The number of women coming back wounded from the Russian front proves that the contingent of the adventurous females on the firing lines is considerable. These women as a general rule cut their hair, assume a soldier's uniform and get away secretly with the connivance of friends among the soldiers. Others start alone on various pretexts, such as seeking injured relatives, and then don male attire when they reach the front."[6]

A number of patriotic schoolgirls also left home without permission to fight for their country. For example, in the spring of 1916, the Russian journal *Novoe Vremya* (New times) reported on twelve Russian schoolgirls who joined the army in August 1914 and continued to fight in the ranks.[7] This type of press coverage, however, did not dissuade the Russian army from curtailing these permissive recruiting practices.

Tatiana Leonidovna Dubinskaya was such a schoolgirl who served as a soldier in 1916. Initially disguised as a male, she fought the Austrians and Germans on the eastern front in Galicia for more than a year, from about the spring of 1916 to the summer of 1917. In 1930 she recounted her personal experiences as a soldier in a novel, based on her experiences, entitled *In the Trenches*, published in Moscow. The book was significant as it reportedly marked the first major account of a female soldier from World War I to be published in Soviet Russia.[8] Dubinskaya subsequently revised and republished a shorter version of her story under a new title, *Machine Gunner*, in 1936.

In the Trenches received critical acclaim when first published, being favorably compared with Erich Maria Remarque's 1929 classic World War I novel, *All Quiet on the Western Front*, which portrayed the stark realism of life in the trenches through the eyes of a young German soldier. Dubinskaya's main character, Zinaida "Zina" Kramskaya, had similar experiences and may likely have been influenced by the style of *All Quiet on the Western Front*. Zina developed close ties to her brothers in arms, endured the hardships and stresses of war, became exposed to the undercurrents of revolutionary thinking in the ranks, and also came to grips with the disruptive effects of the Czar Nicholas II's abdication in March 1917, which led to the wide-scale spread of a socialist revolution in the army.

Zina's story began with her running away from home in Kazan, a major city in European Russia, and joining the Seventy-Fourth Stavropolsky Infantry Regiment of the Twelfth Infantry Division as a scout during the Galicia campaign against the Austrians and Germans. In the course of the campaign, her regiment participated in operations along a wide front from Studzianka (present day Studinka) in the northwest, to Okna in the southwest (currently part of the western Ukraine), spanning approximately two hundred kilometers (see appendix for maps).[9]

After returning home for a visit with her family, where she wrestled with remaining and returning to a normal life, Zina instead found herself drawn back to the theater of war. Back at the front, however, in the wake of a revolution that overthrew the czar and the Romanov dynasty, there were widespread changes sweeping across the army. The revolution brought a provisional socialist government to power whose new policies caused havoc in the army. For example, the new government abolished the death penalty and instituted policies of social equality that undermined discipline. As soldiers no longer feared their officers, soldiers' committees emerged to challenge traditional authority from their officers. All military orders had to be submitted to and approved by the soldiers' committee before being issued to the troops. As traditional discipline broke down, disgruntled soldiers summarily executed unfavorable officers without facing any repercussions. These sudden changes caused a massive destabilization in the army that led many soldiers, including those in Zina's regiment, to desert and return home. Being exposed to revolutionary propaganda in the army, she supported the ideals of defending the lower classes from exploitation by the upper classes, but she was not an ardent revolutionary. Her story ended abruptly in the summer of 1917, in the wake of her regiment retreating and disbanding during a large Austrian counterattack.

The two versions of Dubinskaya's novel have much in common. Most of the characters and much of the storyline remain essentially the same, but there are a few notable exceptions. In *Machine Gunner*, Zina is seventeen when she joins the army, whereas in *In the Trenches*, Zina is fifteen, Dubinskaya's actual age upon joining. *Machine Gunner* also clearly reflects the pressures of Stalin's Russia to produce a more politically acceptable version of her story. The revised story pays more attention to the revolutionary fervor that ushered in the March 1917 revolution and highlights Zina's role as a staunch supporter of the revolutionary cause. As such, Zina and her friends are portrayed as more radicalized than their characters in *In the Trenches*. In *Machine Gunner*, for example, she includes descriptions of witnessing clashes between special shock troops of General Lavr Kornilov, a senior army commander who became a leading anti-Bolshevik after the November 1917 Bolshevik revolution, and her army unit in the summer of 1917 (months before the Bolshevik revolution), which were clearly fabricated to satisfy a Stalinist agenda. The result is a somewhat contrived storyline with a different fictionalized ending than the one portrayed in *In the Trenches*, the later account ending with Zina fighting the forces of General Kornilov rather than returning home to her family and the pursuit of her education.

Relatively little is known about Tatiana Leonidovna Dubinskaya-Krulikovskaya (1902-90). After she left the army in 1917, she served with the Red Army during the Civil War (1917-22) as a soldier with the 7th Caucasian Regiment of the Chervonnogo Cossacks and also as a nurse in a hospital at Vinnytsia in the Ukraine. Following the Civil War, she became a typist for the Red Army in Moscow. She later became a writer. In 1929 she published articles in four issues of *Young Guard* magazine. The following year, she published *In the Trenches.* The Communist Party sent her to Tajikistan in 1931, where, with her third husband, she worked for the party in remote villages and also as a correspondent for Tajikistan's communist newspaper. On her return to Moscow, she became active with the Union of Soviet Writers (which focused on party and state control of literature) after its establishment in 1932, which influenced her to write the revised *Machine Gunner* to better reflect Stalinist ideals. During this time, she also began earning a reputation as a Communist Party informant through her association with famed Russian poet and essayist Osip Mandelstam, who was arrested during the Stalinist repression of the 1930s.[10] Mandelstam's wife later noted:

> Evidently Sargidzhan and his wife had been set to watch us, and they made constant attempts to trap us. His wife especially kept after me to meet some foreigner. That was very dangerous at the time—the winter of 1932–3. Ten times a day they would both come in to see us. The conversations about foreigners went like this: I absolutely had to meet So-and-so because he would give me some stockings. You could get things from foreigners, they could pass things to you, and so on. It was to me that she was forever coming with that sort of thing—she was a very low type. Osya [Osip] understood right away one couldn't talk in the presence of Dubinskaya and Sargidzhan.[11]

Dubinskaya was married four times. Her first husband was a Red Army commander named Grigory Chernyakhovsky, whom she divorced in 1921. They had a son, Yuri, born in 1920. Little is known about her second husband, whose last name was Dubinsky, whom she divorced in 1928. She divorced her third husband, writer Sergei P. Borodin (who wrote under the pseudonym Amir Sargidzhan), in 1936.[12] Little is known about her fourth husband, whose last name was Krulikov, or her life until her death in 1990.

In Dubinskaya's novel her main character, Zinaida Kramskaya, comes from a middle class family in Kazan, is one of three children, and is well educated. Zina's father works at a natural history museum and her family has at least one live-in servant. Zina's brother has been presumably killed in the war. Her older sister lives with her parents. Zina has a love of horses and a desire for adventure. She spends a lot of her spare time visiting a dragoon regiment stationed near her home before she decides to seek adventure by running off to war, where she later becomes a cavalry scout.

In April 1930 the United Press International (UPI) reported that an American publisher had acquired the rights for an English edition of Dubinskaya's novel, but if that was the case, the book never went into print. Russian censorship may have prevented the English edition from appearing. The UPI added that unless Dubinskaya's "startlingly frank narrative" was revised in translation, it would likely have "some difficulty passing the censorship guards."[13]

There are relatively few memoirs in English written by women who fought in the Russian Army in World War I or in the Civil War that followed. These memoirs include Maria Bothchareva's *My Life as a Peasant, Soldier and Exile* (1918), Miss X's *Woman under Fire: Six Months in the Red Army* (1930), Princess Kati Dadeshkeliani's *Princess in Uniform* (1934), Marina Yurlova's *Cossack Girl* (1934) and *Russia Farewell* (1936), and Lul Gardo's *Cossack Fury: The Experiences of a Woman Soldier with the White Russians* (1938).

This revised edition of *In the Trenches* is significant in bringing to light a new source, albeit a novel based on the personal experiences of its author, in English, to add to the limited number of early twentieth-century Russian warrior women writings. The revised edition has been edited using select portions from *Machine Gunner* to provide greater clarity to Dubinskaya's original story. Most of the geographic locations mentioned in the narrative have been identified in endnotes, but there are several cases where it has not been possible to identify these locations. The names of some geographic locations have been modified to their current spellings, which may have varied since World War I. There are several instances in the narrative where Dubinskaya uses a date, but it is unclear whether it is in reference to the Gregorian ("Western") calendar, which Russia adopted in 1918, or the Julian calendar, whose dates were thirteen days later than the Gregorian calendar. Since Dubinskaya's narrative does not follow a strict chronological timeline, but jumps in some places, brief summaries are included before each chapter to provide better context for the reader. Julia Lemberskiy translated both narratives for this project.

IN THE TRENCHES

CHAPTER 1

Zina, a schoolgirl, runs away from home (Kazan) to join the army.
She goes by train with soldiers to Kazatin and then to Brody on
the eastern frontier (captured July 28, 1916), where she is detained
as a boy and put in a cell to be returned home, but she escapes.

The train rushed regiments to the border:

"We're going to war, brothers."

"I left Stepanida with three young ones. She's full of sorrow and not
well. Vasya, my youngest, just turned nine."

"I left and couldn't even wait for a letter from home. My Aksynia
was in her last few days of pregnancy. We're going to war, brothers.
It's not that simple."

"I just bought a young horse at the Tula market, repaired the wagon,
and painted the wheels red. It shines in the sun. My heart aches thinking
of it. I just got married, and now good-bye, my young wife!"

"I didn't finish my business with my brother. Now they'll cheat my
Glasha. The young horse died last spring. Life is very hard without him."

"Guys, why are you all whining? They say the war will end in a few
months."

The soldiers fell asleep after talking for a little while longer.

It was hard to breathe in the train car from all the cheap tobacco
smoke. If only we had a fresh breeze of air!

I heard a person get up and adjust the train door.

"The wind blows in the morning; it's cold," says a voice.

Another voice says: "Have you frozen? It has been long enough since you slept without your woman. Why are you closing the door, there's no air in here anyway."

They lay down. The door stayed open.

))⟩

Morning; it's time to come out of the caves we made called beds. Bodies ache because of the uncomfortable sleeping positions. I couldn't stay here any longer. What's meant to be, will be. I decided to crawl out from under the bunk bed.

"This is an unexpected turn! What is it?" someone asked.

I wasn't surprised by this question. In reality, I was some little creature with a huge medicine bag.

"Where did you come from?" inquired another.

"I'm, I'm Sergey. I'm fifteen, take me with you to the war. Please take me with you, I'm begging you. Let me go with you. I want to be a soldier," I pleaded.

"What do we need him for, guys? Kick him off!" shouted a soldier.

"Drop it, Mitrich, just let him come. Maybe he will be of use," said another.

"From a glance, he's kind of like my Peter; his face doesn't look like Peter's, but his body looks just like my son's. Let him come along!" said a third soldier.

They gave me tea. One of the soldiers untied his backpack, took out a homemade pretzel, and gave it to me.

A small station; everyone leaped out of the train. The soldiers loosened their belts and everyone went in different directions. Hopping over a stream, I ran to the nearest bushes in sight. Darn! The place was already occupied. I changed my direction.

The soldier's face had a naive smile. "What happened, there's not enough room?" he asked.

))⟩

There were kettles filled with soup on the floor of the train. There was a thick steam coming from them. Everyone gathered around in a circle, sitting cross-legged, indulging themselves in the aromatic soup.

"Here! Eat up!" someone said.

Taking a spoon out of his boot, a blond, freckled soldier handed it to me. I was hungry, but that disgusting spoon spoiled my appetite. I pulled out a pocket knife and turning away from the soldier, I skimmed the spoon with it.

"What are you picking at? That spoon was a gift. My mother gave it to me," he said.

"Stop it," I said. I was embarrassed. Blushing and burning my tongue with the hot soup, I ate in silence. Never at home did I eat with such an appetite as I did that time; I was very hungry.

I slept on the bunk beds again the second night. The soldier, apparently thinking I was cold, kept covering me with a long coat. It was hot. I kicked off the coat.

"Sleep; what's with all the tossing and turning?" he asked.

)))

Kazatin station; there was a crowd of people on the platform.[1] A tall officer with fat cheeks and an orange face walked through the rows of soldiers. He was the general. He walked toward our train car and spoke with the soldiers, who abruptly ended their conversations. He concluded his speech saying: "To our faith, our czar, Our Motherland, under God, my soldiers, to the front lines!" And with a somewhat crooked smile, picking up his hand, with a hoarse voice he screamed, "Hooray!"

A voice was heard breaking through the crowd: "Dearest ones, where are you off to?"

The train slowly rolled away. The general was surrounded by officers, and soldiers lined up to the right and left of them. The orchestra played. The wheels turned faster. The general was no longer in sight. The train moved farther and farther away.

)))

They unloaded us at the Brody station after a five-day journey.[2] Marching through the center of the dirty town, the companies stopped at a big, gray building. At the gate there was a sign, "Central Command of the Army." Here the soldiers impatiently waited for the next marching orders. Finally officers emerged from the doors, and there was a command: "Line up by the order of your numbers!" And the troops resumed marching.

Crowds of boys, forming groups near the Third Regiment, with which I walked, drove me to despair.

The soldiers were delayed a little when passing by the town commandant. Again the boys surrounded me. A captain with a mustache walked over to our company and told the company commander: "Lieutenant, this will not do. It's forbidden for any volunteer boys to tag along with any regiment. They create obstacles. Send him home tomorrow."

I couldn't hold back my tears. My hands were shaking as I tried to open the first aid kit. I pulled out the first bandage I touched. I blew my nose. So this is what I needed my first wound bandage for!

⟩⟩⟩

A woman sat on a single bed in the prison cell. She took a tin cup and splashed water onto a red handkerchief. She touched the handkerchief to a bright bruise under her eye. She had a brown shawl wrapped around her head, tightly tied at her chin. Her rag of a dress barely covered her pale, white body. She looked at me, and reaching into her front pocket, pulled out some crumpled cigarettes with cardboard holders, and offered me a smoke; I refused. Her bottom lip protruded as she spoke: "They say you're the girl that thinks she's getting to the front lines. Humph! The officers always need a girl that sleeps around."

All of a sudden she swung her feet up and, finding a comfortable spot on my knees, stared up at me with dim eyes.

"Soooo! How pleasant and comfortable. Sit there and don't move, like manure in a ditch," she said.

I sat there strained. I was afraid to move. I was afraid to breathe. She smelled bad. Her worn-out, dirty, black shoes were falling off her feet. She turned on her side and placed her palm on her swollen eye, and then with a groan she fell asleep. I wasn't afraid of her anymore. I wanted to stroke her light hair. Where was she from? Who hurt her beautiful eyes?

In the corridor, someone's quick footsteps were heard and then silence again. I don't know how many seconds, minutes, or hours passed. It seemed as if time had stopped. I was thirsty. Thirst burned my throat. The tin cup was on the floor, and the woman's handkerchief covered her. Should I move the sleeping woman's head from my lap? Should I get the water and drink? But I didn't want to disturb the sleep of this stranger; it was a pity to wake her. The handkerchief made a shadow on her tightly shut eyes and the bruise. There was a strange circle at the base of her long eyelashes. I took a good look. It felt like something brushed my back. Strange bugs sank into her skin by her beautiful eyelashes. One of these monsters detached itself for a moment, and changing its position, again sank itself into her skin. The woman flailed her arm and moved the scarf on her head. There was fuzz on her hair that stuck out. Her eyebrows were raised a little bit, her nose covered in little pimples, and under it, a thin, dry layer of mucus. The knots on her worn-out and tied-up shoelaces were stained with white paint. There was a pretty, orange piece of cloth tied on her ripped stocking under her skirt. When she opened her dry mouth, she smacked her tongue, and groaning, turned on her side. As she slightly picked her head up, I bent down to get the water, and when I brought it to my lips, there was a sharp blow against my elbow. The water spilled all over the place.

"Don't drink that, girl, I'm walking around with syphilis!"

She struck a match and lit a cigarette. The room filled with smoke.

There were quick footsteps in the hallway, and then a boy was shoved into our cell with the words, "We'll show you. Making fun of the officers, we'll cut your tongue off, you little devil." The boy shook his head and smiled. The door slammed shut.

"What's your name?" he asked.

"Zina," I replied.

"Why are you dressed as a soldier?"

"I am going to the front lines."

"You are a girl, they will not let you fight. What's her name?"

"I don't know."

"You are in here together, and you don't know her name?"

"My name is Anna Phillipovna," replied the woman.

"Why do you have a bruise under your eye?" he asked.

"That doesn't concern you," she answered.

"Zina, who is going to give you a gun?" he asked.

"The commander," I said.

"Do the commanders make the guns themselves?" he asked.

"No, they make them at the factories," I said.

"I made my own, and I'm not sharing. But I didn't feud with the Germans, so I'm not shooting at them either," he remarked.

"Who are you going to shoot at?" I asked.

"At the dogs, if they are rabid," he stated.

Someone knocked on the cell door and said: "To the station, off to the staging post, step to it, poor rats."

The boy stood, straightened up, and teasingly placed his little, dirty palm to his temple, saluting the soldier.

"All right then, let's go, governor," said the soldier.

Just as we walked out the boy made a run for it down the nearest path. The escorts all chased him. Taking advantage of the chaos, I ran to the nearest gates of some house and crawled into the corner of a garden. Only at sunrise did I separate myself from the corn growing around me. I thought of the woman who was with me in my cell. Why didn't she run with me? Doesn't she care about her life?

CHAPTER 2

Zina joins a frontline scout unit, the First Battalion, Third Company, Fourth Platoon, Seventy-Fourth Stavropolsky Infantry Regiment, Twelfth Division, in their reserve trenches in Galicia in the summer of 1916. As they march to the front, they pass refugees on their way to Zastavki, a western Ukrainian village, where they occupy frontline trenches.

I lived in a trench dugout with two scouts, Sasha Gusev and Trofim Terekhin. Sasha had blond, curly hair, dark eyebrows, and his eyes were the bluest-blue. We had lunch. Sasha licked his bright lips that were the color of ripe raspberries and wiped the sweat from his forehead. He undid the top button of his uniform, from which you could see his red Russian folk shirt, and got up from the nightstand he was sitting on. Moving his arms, he spread his broad shoulders.

"Sasha, hide the embroidery. You'll be in trouble if our company commander sees it, and hide the lacing too," said Trofim. His face was brown, as if he'd been born tan. His unkempt beard and his hair, black as soil, made Sasha's blond curls stand out even more. Trofim ate his porridge, got up from the bunk, and started praying, all the while making a cross on his chest. Sasha watched him, smirking, and hid the black cord that was normally used as a belt with folk dancing clothes. He pulled down his army shirt, and the belt was now hidden under it.

"Why did you come here? You think it's fun?" Trofim asked. "Sometimes you get so tired, it's such fatigue, it feels like all your bones are breaking, and without any sleep, such exhaustion. Sometimes you just walk around like you're drunk. And then look here, it's the commander; you didn't give your salute, so then he smacks you in the face so hard you faint. No, boy, you should have stayed home. You obviously don't have to work at home, your hands look too well taken care of!"

My heart ached with thoughts of home. How is my mother now? How did she react to my running away, I thought. I remembered her thoughtful, dark-gray eyes and smoothly combed, black hair collected into a big bun on her head. Mother was busy not only with us, but father's earnings weren't enough, and so she gave music lessons. My sister, Valya, always sick and frail, was at times afraid of me, even though she was three years older than me. It wasn't hard for me to pick her up with the strength of a giant, squeeze her, throw her on my back, and toss her aside. And father? An image of my father, who worked at a museum, stood vividly before my eyes. His office had a big, green table and books, manuscripts, and a large number of test tubes. My father would open a test tube, take out something, and carefully place it on the table. A butterfly—again he would take a test tube, repeatedly examine a butterfly, and after that he would fasten it onto a pin. My father had a lot of containers and bottles that contained solutions, and there were bugs in the solutions. My father used to spend his days in his office writing something. Sometimes when I would come in he would sit next to me on the couch, and he would always ask me the same question: "So how are things, Zinaedische?"[1] Then he would smoke his giant pipe and offer me dark Bavarian beer, which was always under the desk. I remember when I was about six, and everyone in the house had left, leaving me in my father's care. Clearly he was very busy that evening. Like all children, I was very curious. At first my father was very patient with all of my questions, and then he got sick of them and just didn't have the time to attend to all sorts of explanations. He offered me beer. I didn't really like beer, but I liked the process of it being poured. It foamed so interestingly! Going unnoticed by my father, little by little, I kept filling up my cup with beer and drank with little sips. I kept pouring, it kept foaming, and I was amused. Repeating this process a few times, I got drunk and fell asleep, which rid father of any other necessary caregiving. But in the morning, I disappeared from the office, being embarrassed that the leather couch was soaked.

I got really sad with memories of my father. I quickly got up and walked out of the dugout.

The clanging of pots and scraping of shovels made noise. The soldiers were hectic. They were saddling the horses. The captain's carriage approached our dugout with such fanfare as if it were the arrival of a king. The old colonel was departing, and everyone was gathering. It was less than an hour before the colonel returned from the regimental headquarters at the village of Gai.[2] They gave him a saddled horse, and what a beautiful horse it was! Oh, if I could only get to ride a horse, I thought! I loved horses and, even before I was eight, I rode very well. Sasha walked up to me and said that we were leaving our reserve positions for the front lines.

The soldiers were in position. I was part of the Fourth Platoon of the Third Company. The rain poured, making mud of the sticky dirt, and feet were slipping in all directions. I didn't want to fall behind. I wanted to follow them. I had a great desire to see the positions where the soldiers hid to shoot from and to see what goes on in war. We walked for five *versts* without stopping.[3] Finally we started slowing down and stopped for a small break. The soldiers barely had a chance to light their cigarettes when the sergeant gave the command: "And up!" The soldiers gathered and began lining up again. Trofim had a swollen cheek, probably a swollen tooth, and he hardly took his hand off it.

"Are we going to march for much longer?" Trofim asked resentfully, pressing his overcoat to his cheek to warm it. He kept on mumbling, "What are you getting involved for, things are fine without you." Picking up the edge of his coat, he wiped his nose.

There were wagons of refugees traveling along the high road to the left of the regiment. The horses barely walked, tripping over themselves. The wagons were filled with washtubs, buckets, pillows and blankets, exhausted faces of women, and disinterested gazes of men. Women sat on top of the wagons, while the men walked on with their heads bent down. In front, a baby cried while sucking on its mother's breast.

"Atta! Atta!" a boy screamed and hit the horses with a stick. Mustering their last strength, the spotted horses move forward. "Atta! Atta!" again screamed the dark-eyed boy, and just as he was raising his hand to hit the horse, it collapsed. The seven-year-old boy jumped up, and the boy's mother got up just as quickly from the carriage. The horse lay there motionless. It just turned its head and gazed at her and let out a long neigh. The boy, without letting the stick out of his hand, scratched the back of his head and, with a lost expression on his face, stared at his mother. The mother, pressing her tight lips together, started to unsaddle the horse. The soldiers helped her pull the horse into a ditch.

The mother came up to the carriage, took her baby and dark-eyed son, and they walked away abandoning all their belongings. Behind them, stumbling, walked a lonely horse.

)))

For some time, I kept up with the army, but I felt that my legs were too heavy, either from weariness or the oversized boots they gave me. My feet just kept moving around inside those boots, big, huge, monstrous boots. If I were to take them off, they would probably all laugh. I had to take it.

We walked a lot and rested very little. I didn't look for a spot to rest anymore. My legs felt significantly worse after sitting a little. They would get even heavier. It felt like one hundred pounds of dirt stuck to them. I barely dragged them along.

"You walking, lil' boy?" said the approaching sergeant. His face was covered in smallpox scars, that's why the soldiers gave him the nickname of "crater." He walked by the back rows and yelled: "Widerrr marrrch! Thirrrrd Company, puull up!" Easy for you to say, I thought, your boots fit you perfectly. I looked at him with jealousy and resentment, as if it were his fault that my boots were so big.

It got dark. The regiment walked on. We walked through the fields of Galicia, through the moonlit cemeteries. Some peasants walked home late. Their long, white shirts cast shadows on the crosses.

We went up a hill. The lights became visible. The village was close. People swayed from fatigue like a grandfather clock. Trofim cursed every minute: "I don't like this. You can't compare it with the way we fought at Przemyśl, and right now what do we do?[4] Dig trenches in the dirt all the time."

We came to the village of Zastavki.[5] We heard a voice, "Placement officers, you sons of bitches, take care of the companies!"

The gates opened, and the eight of us walked in. Suddenly awakened by guests of the night, a dog pulled on his chain, struggling to breathe. He barked furiously. I went to the barn. I took off my boots and lit a match. There was a huge blister on my foot. I'll see what happens tomorrow, I thought. Right then I just couldn't concentrate and, just like a falling tree, I fell onto the straw straight to sleep.

I woke up. Bright rays of sunlight peeked in through the cracks of the barn. My body felt heavy, as if everything was filled up with mercury. It was hard to pick up my arms. I still had that blister on my foot. I had to get rid of it. I had to get rid of it no matter what happened! I immediately decided to cut it. I cleaned the little knife that I had and cut into the blister. The effect was immediate; the blister popped and a murky liquid poured out. I wiped the dirt away with my spit, and then I wrapped my foot in a clean cloth.[6] I tried to put on my boot, it hurt to walk, but it was better than the day before. I didn't always wash my feet here before bed, but at home I wouldn't have been allowed to go to bed without doing so. The rain washed my feet here, and I got stronger. I could probably have picked up Valya with one hand. I glanced at myself in a little mirror, my face was tan. If only my family could see me now.

"Hey, Sergey, why are you staring at yourself? Enough, pack your things. You're a winner kid. Do you know how far we walked?—thirty versts. When it gets dark we will move to our new positions."

Sasha interrupted my thoughts. I threw my backpack over my shoulder and left.

)))

"Get rid of that cigarette, stop smoking!"

The companies slowly, quietly walked along the valley. There was a piercing whistle in my ear.

"Sergey, get down! There's a bullet. Get down!" warned Sasha.

"Why should I get down?" I asked. Sasha didn't answer me. Without analyzing what I was doing, I walked bending over. There was a ray of light in front of me. At first it was thin, and then it got wider and wider. Sasha pulled my sleeve, and we fell headfirst.

"Where is the light from? Why did we fall? Sasha?" I called.

"I don't have time for you. Look, the Austrian searchlight. Lie there and be quiet. If he gets a feel for you, he will hit you with a shell," Sasha explained.

"Sasha, is the shell big?" I asked.

"I just told you to be quiet!" he replied sharply.

"Sasha, is the war still far away?" I asked.

"Shut up!" he shouted.

I moved closer to him just in case. There was a blow, and I felt like the ground underneath us shook. I got scared from Sasha's terrifying words and the stirrings around me. Maybe I should turn back? Run away? No, I am going to go with them. Isn't Sasha a person just like me? It doesn't matter that he is a man. He had a head and arms and legs. I straightened out, but at the same moment there was a sharp sound above my head and crashing down, it lit up in flames. I fell again.

"Sasha, I'm scared," I cried out.

"Wait, it gets worse. The German isn't stupid. He managed to shoot up the whole field. Lie there quietly now. You too, Sergey. See, he aimed correctly, we could be next," Sasha warned.

Something whistled, whined, and whisking right passed our heads, blew up. Well there it was, a shell, I thought. The soldiers got down, then stood up and got down again. We advanced.

"Ow . . . ow . . . fight . . . ow . . ." Someone was injured. It hit the First Platoon. The valley got quiet. Then there were people running past us. They bent over the wounded man. The explosions stopped. The company stayed down for a little then got up, ran quickly, and got down again.

"That's the communications trench, which means we've arrived," said Trofim.[7]

Trofim walked up to us. We walked into a dark corridor and continued in single file. My hand was feeling around, the dirt was falling. Putting my hand lower, I felt the ground, and it slipped unpleasantly under my fingers. As soon as I took my hand away, I was tempted to put it back. Again the dirt started to slip under my hand and tickle me. Worms! It was scary and disgusting. I didn't want to go here. I wouldn't go any farther.

"What's with you? You're being stubborn like a bull. Why are you so set against walking forward? The fire ceased. Why did you get scared?" said a voice. Someone pushed me from behind. I started walking again. We turned right. It was wider here, more spacious in the nighttime darkness and a barely distinguishable silhouette of a soldier bent over something.

"Trofim, what's that hole there? What are the soldiers doing there?" I asked.

"That's no hole, it's a gun port. That's how you fire from the trenches," he answered.

))）

In the trenches, beside me, Sasha, and Trofim, sat two more scouts, Chereshenko and Zaporozhets, who were good friends. They came from a little village in Poltava Gubernia and were amazingly alike.[8] Their flowing mustaches were exactly alike in form, except Zaporozhets had thick hair, and Chereshenko had thin hair. Chereshenko's height made him stand out. He stood out not only between him and his friend, but among the whole regiment. There was no giant like him. Sitting in the dugout, he had to bend very, very low. When they spoke to anyone, Zaporozhets and Chereshenko were always smiling, showing the few teeth that they had, and as if they planned it, they both twirled their big mustaches.

Trofim took off his overcoat and threw it to me, saying:

"Here, Sergey, sleep. You were scared out there in the valley tonight. The German is opposite us, there is no other way. It's always like that, silent as a grave. The Austrian is different, he is restless. He will open fire several times a night, but the German, he doesn't fear us. With the

German, you always have to keep your guard up. Guys, it's time for us to take our guard duty posts."

All four of them got up and walked out of the dugout. I was left alone. A small candle was flickering out. It was quiet, and I couldn't sleep. I kept thinking, how can I finally tell them that I'm not a boy? It's really uncomfortable playing the role of a boy, it's hard in conversation. Why should I even hide it? Isn't it all the same? I was too overwhelmed by everything that happened this evening. What if the Germans come now? Germans seemed really scary and intimidating to me. I was scared of them. I wanted to go search for Sasha. I couldn't sit here alone. I extinguished the candle and walked out. It was ghastly walking through these trenches. I kept thinking that I'm going to walk a few steps and fall into one of those deep ditches, like I read about at home. Shuffling my feet, I slowly moved them, creeping through, feeling the ground with one foot. People weren't visible; I heard only voices, but the voices were so muffled. What if I stumbled upon the Austrians or the Germans? Who the hell knows where this is leading!

"Hey, who's there?" I screamed.

My own voice seemed impressive. I wasn't so scared anymore. Gaining courage, I kept walking.

"What are you shouting for? Do you think you are at home or something?" asked a soldier.

The soldier walked me to our dugout. I lit the candle, and he reached into his pocket. He pulled out a rumpled-up piece of paper, a thin envelope covered with black dots and a small pencil.

"They say you are quite literate. Write me a letter to send home and write big, so it's legible, but write everything as I say it." He dictated:

Dearest Mother and Father,

I send you my best regards, and to my sister, Praskovia, and my younger brother, Mitka, the deepest regards. To our godfather, Egoru Nikitichu, send him my regards, and tell him that I received the cream he sent me for back pain. As soon as we get off for leave, I will bring him back the cream. Also, dearest mother, please send my regards to Agrippina Vassilievna, who always stands out at church and sings so compassionately. You'll notice her right away. She always walks around wearing a pink blouse and green skirt, like the grass in our garden. Do you know that I like her? Father, send me news of what they say about the war. Check on what they say about when it will end. I am tired of fighting on the front lines, it makes my insides turn. The lice are merciless, and they walk all over our bodies as if they were at home. I wish you health and hope you flourish. Like a bird waits for spring, I wait for your response. Tell me, did you sell our cow Katie? Once again, I send my best regards to you and everyone who is related to us by blood. Mother, again I turn to you and ask you please don't forget to say hello to Agrippina Vassilievna. I'm going to write her soon. I am healthy and stay faithful in my feelings to you. Your loyal son, unfortunate and miserable in the trenches, Aleksei.

Finished with the letter, I put it into the envelope and gave it to the soldier, who remarked: "Listen, boy, did you write everything exactly the way I said it? As soon as we get into the German trenches, I will get you an officer's flannel undershirt."

I told the soldier I wrote everything just as he said it.

"Well, on that note, thank you. I'm going on guard duty. It's time," he replied. He put the letter inside his shirt and left.

I walked around the Fourth Platoon trenches during the day. Close by stood four run-down houses with no roofs and windows that looked like the vacant eyes of a skull. In the distance, anywhere you looked there was uneven land. I could see the line of Austro-German trenches. To the far right of the battalion, the trenches were made in zigzags. Not one living thing, no one would show their face above the trenches. Only not far from me, a jackdaw sat calmly on a tiny hill. There was a loud noise and whistling, an artillery shell landed near the Eighth Company. It made a lot of dust, but didn't explode. I hid in the communications trench.

I walked to my company. I was going to learn how to shoot a rifle. The soldiers were placed far apart, about fifteen to twenty paces apart from each other. I figured I would ask that one, with the orange beard; I knew him, his name was Vaciliy Klimich. For some reason, the visor of his hat was pulled all the way down to his nose, and he held the cord of his red tobacco pouch with his teeth. He rolled a long cigarette, neatly rolled up his tobacco pouch, and shoved it into his coat pocket, which was sprawled on the ground. He adjusted his service cap insignia and started smoking.

There was an officer walking out of the communications trench towards us. I recognized him from the wagon train. The lieutenant had on a brown shirt and on his chest he wore the St. Vladimir Order, which he fiddled with, using his right hand, keeping his left hand in his pocket.[9] He whistled as he walked. His boots were shined to perfection. He wore blue trousers, unlike the other officers who wore them in khaki. He walked up to Klimich, grabbed his rifle, and aimed it. He turned red, and his hands turned into fists as he shouted: "You bearded ass! Your sights are wrong. You're shooting at nothing and wasting bullets!"

"Sir, what are you hitting me for? You're young enough to be my son," Klimich exclaimed.

"Silence, you shaggy wretch!" shouted the officer. The officer swung back his arm and hit him again. Klimich was shaken. He sat down on the steps.

"Get up, you orange-haired bastard! Don't you know how to talk to an officer?"

The lieutenant abruptly turned towards me. I looked at him and was unbelievably amazed by his eyes. They looked like glass. I had never seen such colorless eyes before. His big nose had a bump, and his really thin lips and those eyes, those unpleasant eyes, reminded me of some predatory bird. The officer looked at me.

"Why aren't you occupied, you little brat?" asked the lieutenant.

"It's not nice to fight," I replied.

"Get the hell out of here, and I don't want to see you again," he warned me.

I walked away. When the lieutenant walked away, I came back to Vaciliy Klimich. He was wiping the blood from his nose with his tobacco pouch.

"You see, boy, how he hit me? You saw how he hit me there, friend? That's elegant Lieutenant Zambor. All he ever does is ride in the wagon train, but when he appears, he always tries to beat you up. And what are we suffering for? The son of a bitch broke my cigarette. Now I have nothing to smoke."

)))

The whole line was silent. Rarely would you hear a lonely gunshot. Not far from the squad commander's dugout, on the hill, were a few of the sergeant's men. Bending over, apparently attentively looking at something, they straightened their backs from time to time and laughed loudly. Noticing my nearing, they waved their hands.

"Hurry up and you can play around with us too!" someone said.

There was a piece of paper being held down on the corners by rocks, and there was a silver five-kopeck coin on it. A soldier untied a handkerchief and took out a very unpleasant louse with a fat belly and let it go on the paper. His neighbor did the same.

"Whose will it be, whose will it be? He is walking pretty fast, mine got it! Race it!"

The winner took the coin, and another one was placed for bidding. The game continued.

)))

Sasha stood near the dugout, and there was a pot filled with water in front of him. He filled his mouth with the water, so that his cheeks swelled up, and then he would spit it out. While washing his face, he took off a peacock-embroidered towel that was wrapped around him and wiped his face. He looked at himself in a mirror, brushed his curls, and began to sing: "Don't fly blond curls."

"Where have you been?" he asked me.

"I was learning how to shoot, and Vaciliy Klimich was teaching me," I said.

"Well, did you learn?" he asked.

"I learned," I replied.

"You're not lying?" he asked.

"Ask him yourself if you don't believe me," I said.

"Sergey, to tell you the truth, it's rare that we shoot our rifles. Did you see how hard the First Company was hit today? he asked.

"I saw, but oh, I saw, I saw, I wanted to run there. They say that there's a lot of wounded and dead there, but I was scared to go without you."

"You were scared, scared, yeah it's easy to get you scared, Sergey. You're going to die of fear. Did you see the German prisoner? He gave himself up. The battalion commander asked him, what regiment are you from? But he was silent, didn't say a word. They took him to the regimental headquarters."

Sasha looked at himself in the mirror again, fingered his hair, wrapped the mirror in a handkerchief and put it in his pocket.

"Guys, get up, the division commander is walking through the trenches with the chief of staff," Zaporozhets announced.

"Why the hell did he come? This never happens," someone stated.

"The division commander, he's a general," Zaporozhets added.

Zaporozhets, conveying the news and struggling for air, ran on.

"Let's go see, Sergey," said Sasha.

All of a sudden I had the urge to tell Sasha that I wasn't a boy, and yet again I held myself back and stayed quiet. No, let him find out for himself, can they all really not tell?

"Look, Sergey, that tall one, he's the brave division commander, General Mitchvolodov. Next to him is Captain Melnikov, the one without the hand, he is a temporary battalion commander; ours is Captain Krapivansky. He should come back soon, he's injured. Captain Krapivansky is so brave. He is very polite and respectful to us soldiers."

Thin, tall, in a black hat, with his *bashlik* carelessly about his shoulders and the spurs on his boots rattling softly, stood the general.[10] He would touch a white handkerchief to his gray mustache, and his eyes squinted every minute. He said something to the chief of staff, Colonel Neymirok, who stood next to him, heavyset and wallowing as he walked, like a duck, who kept jotting down notes in a notepad. Captain Melnikov, pressing his lips together, with his one hand, showed the general the gun ports. Behind them, walking with small footsteps, Colonel Svirsky, the regimental commander, caught up to the general.

"Colonel, who is this person?" asked the general.

"Sir, this is our Sergey. We took him as a volunteer. Will you let him stay?" the colonel asked.

I froze in anticipation and somehow straightened my back. The general looked me over from head to toe, over and over again. He looked at my breast and squinted his eyes.

"You can keep him; an interesting specimen. I will have to get to know him. Send him to the division headquarters for a visit. We will take a picture of him," replied the general.

)))

Trofim got sick. He had a fever. The company commander let him stay at the officers' quarters.

"Well, Sergey, let's go. I will walk you to the village. The regimental commander told me to take you to the division headquarters this morning. Don't forget how I taught you to stand in front of the general," Trofim said.

Klimich walked into the dugout.

"Well hello. How are you, Trofim? Is it really true that something terrible happened? Where are you going? Sergey, you look like a young apple, but your hair needs to be cut a little. Give me the buzzer, Sasha, I will fix him up in a second," remarked Klimich.

The procedure with the hair didn't last long.

"Where are you off to?" asked Klimich again.

Sasha explained to him.

"All right, don't stay too long with the general. Come back. You're not a bad fellow," Klimich added.

CHAPTER 3

Zina visits General Mitchvolodov, the division commander, at
division headquarters, who discovers her to be a girl. She asks
permission to stay as a soldier, and he agrees, subsequently issuing
orders that reveal her as a young woman. She is exposed to the war
firsthand. She sees her first wounded soldiers, and she goes on her
first combat mission, a reconnaissance of the Austrian lines, where
she experiences the fear of getting caught on the enemy barbed
wire and temporarily separated from her unit. Her regimental
commander advises her that her family wants her to return home,
but she chooses to stay.

"Excuse me, your Excellency. I brought a visitor," said a lieutenant.

The door flew open. The general moved the stool on which his feet
were resting and got up from the bed.

"Please, do come in. Lieutenant, you are dismissed. Well, Sergey,
that's the name, if I'm not mistaken, right?" asked the general.

I looked at the general, and he looked at me. I tried to stand up
straight in front of him as Trofim taught me. This time he wasn't looking me up and down, but instead he was staring straight at my breast.
I stood in the same position, first looking up, then averting my eyes. I
felt myself blush. I looked at the general. It lasted a second, but it felt
like an eternity. The general stared, stared and squinted. One thing
was certain, what I was able to hide from the soldiers for so long, I
wasn't able to hide from the general.

He walked up to me, took me by the shoulders, and bent down to my ear, and said, "You're a girl? Name?"

I answered him just as quietly: "Zinaida, sir. I have a request, let me stay in the regiment."

The general lifted my chin and pulled me closer and said, "You could get killed, child." Then with a decisive tone, "All right I will give the orders to the regiment. They will receive it as an order."

Then his voice got soft again.

"Come to the camp, I will be waiting for you. Will you come?" he asked.

My muscles were tense, and I was slouching my shoulders. I put my hand on my hat.

"Yes, sir, I ask for permission to go back to the regiment now," I replied.

General Mitchvolodov asked again whether I would come. He got really close to my face and breathed on me. He smelled of gingerbread, cake, chocolate, and cologne. He squeezed my chin, hugged me, and let me go, saying: "Go on, girl, they will drive you."

I walked quickly without looking back. I felt a terrible loneliness. I felt like something extremely heavy would collapse on me at any moment. I sat down in a wagon. The horse moved. I wrapped my hands around my head, rocking back and forth with my whole body. I closed my eyes, and my heart pounded. I had a very bad feeling. I wanted to get to the dugout as quickly as possible to Sasha, Trofim, and Klimich. I had to tell them everything. I thought that they would understand everything, and I wouldn't have to go to the division headquarters anymore. Trofim and Sasha, they wear gray overcoats, clumsy boots, their shirts are usually dirty, but even still, they are not as mean as the officers. Why did Mitchvolodov pinch me?

)))

I was going to Klimich, and I walked into male nurses carrying stretchers.

"Oh, brothers, oh, dearest, hurry, carry me to the station, hurry carry me!" a wounded soldier pleaded.

The nurses stopped and slowly put the stretchers down and lit up cigarettes. I bent over the wounded.

"Sonny, hey, sonny, help me out," called one of the wounded.

The Austrian artillery fired persistently and with deafening noise all day. That was the first day I saw so many wounded up close. The soldier's shirt and his undershirt were cut up into pieces. The blood was pouring out of a hole in his side. The soldier groaned.

"Dearest, help me up, maybe it will ease the pain," he pleaded.

I tried my best, pulling him by the shoulder.

"Ow, ow! Sweetheart, just put me down, don't touch me," he yelled. I carefully let go of the soldier.

Someone carried another soldier. His head was wrapped, but his gauze was soaked in blood. He seemed dead. The blood was dried up. He let out a muffled cry and opened his eyes. He flailed his arm and then dropped it helplessly. Again he repeated the gesture, as if he were trying to take the bandage off his head. The nurse threw me a bandage, saying, "Here, tie him up a fresh bandage; you see the gauze dried up, and it's irritating his wound."

My hands were shaking; I tried to unwrap the bandage. I took the absorbent cotton off and opened the wound, and there were pieces of brain on it. Everything became hazy, and everything spun. I felt nauseous. Horror washed over me.

"Mit, hey, Mit, he can't tie the bandage. He lost his nerve. Ugh, you piece of shit, move!" shouted a nurse.

The nurse ripped off a clean piece of gauze, took the brains off the cotton, and put them back into the soldier's head. He bandaged up the soldier's wound again.

"He won't live. It's pointless to keep carrying him," the nurse complained.

They got up and trudged away.

Others came with stretchers and behind them our battalion commander was on one. They stopped and quietly put down the stretchers. They thoroughly wiped the sweat from their foreheads. I saw the familiar face of Captain Melnikov.

"Pick him up, guys, pick him up. Why did you stop, the wound isn't small, but remember, don't give him a drop of water on the way," a nurse cautioned.

The one-handed Melnikov was wounded in the stomach. Later we found out that even though there were strict orders not to give him any liquids, his servant, Shecter, gave him vodka from the flask he carried around. The severely wounded captain ate sausage and to the disbelief of the doctors, got better.

"So, how are things, kid?" Captain Melnikov asked me. "Be careful, so you don't get hurt. Don't walk around the trenches if you don't have to. The trenches are easy to shoot at. It's hard to escape it. Why don't you go into a dugout?"

)))

"I'm going to go check, guys," said Sasha.

I eagerly jumped up and followed him.

"What's with you? Sit here, I don't know how I'm going to get across myself, those devils are shooting up the whole field. Don't go," warned Sasha.

Sasha wouldn't take me with him.

I kept imagining Captain Melnikov and the wounded soldiers I saw that day. My curiosity disgusted me. Who do I think I am? I came here, and I wasn't even doing anything. I should find something for myself to do and stop this stupid behavior acting like a boy. That day I had to tell them I was a girl. I seemed like a coward to myself, because I didn't have the courage to tell them the truth.

"Here, you, read this!" Sasha angrily remarked. He came back mad, he didn't look at me. I took the paper he held out and read it:

MILITARY ORDER NO.2
(Seventy-Fourth Stavropolsky Infantry Regiment)

ITEM 1
The commander of the First Battalion, Captain Melnikov, is on
leave due to injury.

ITEM 2

Commander of the First Company, Captain Krapivansky, is now designated the commander of the First Battalion.

ITEM 3

Lieutenant Yerosh, after coming back from the infirmary, will take command of the First Company.

ITEM 4

Volunteer Shansky is placed under arrest for ten days for his unjustified absence from his command, which he will serve in the regiment's military jail.

ITEM 5

Volunteer Zinaida Kramskaya (who is Sergey) of the Third Company, will have all the allowances and duties of a soldier, part of the infantry scouts.

Well there it was! The general fulfilled my wish. I looked at Sasha, he looked at me, but his head was bent.

"Sasha, don't be mad," I said.

"Why should I be mad, it's not your mother's fault she gave birth to a daughter instead of a son," he replied.

"Sasha, take me with you on reconnaissance duty. Let's go now," I said.

"You don't go on reconnaissance during the day, only if the regiment is in action. But now, if you do so much as peek out, they'll definitely get you," he warned.

Both of us were quiet, but not for long. Sasha didn't take his eyes off me.

"You fooled us pretty good. How could we have missed it? You really look like a boy. Whatever; all right, sleep for now, I'll wake you up later. Today we have to cut the enemy's barbed wire, and you're coming with us," he affirmed.

)))

"Hello, Sergey, oh, I forgot it's Zina now, right?" Trofim asked.

"Trofim, I am going on reconnaissance duty with you guys," I commented.

"Oh stop it, don't take her, Sasha. You will die of fright, Zina," he cautioned.

"He already promised me. I am going. How come you can go, and I can't?" I asked.

"Do you think we are going of our own free will? Who wants to go face death by their own free will?" Sasha replied.

"And the war?" I asked.

"What about the war? We aren't fighting for our own wealth. The officers won't let you go, but if you want, come with us," he answered.

)))

We crawled to the enemy's barbed wire. My heart pounded from fear, and yet something pulled me toward the danger. Shells were exploding, I was scared, but at the same time I was amused by the catlike crawling we were doing through the night. Not too far away, a shell exploded—I moved forward, although I could easily have turned back and hidden in a trench. I stayed in the open space, and I was so proud of my bravery. My bravery was so pleasing! A shrapnel shell exploded—it didn't reach its destination![1] Amazing! It was hard to crawl, I kept hitting clumps of dirt, and the clay on the ground stuck to my body.

"Zina, go left, there's a ditch here!" Trofim warned, as he crawled away from me.

"Hey, Sasha, my stomach hurts, I can't crawl like this anymore," I answered.

"Don't crawl on your stomach, crawl on your side. It might be easier. Shh, shh, we're going through the barbed wire," Sasha cautioned.

I was sweating, so I undid my shirt collar. A bullet whizzed past. A second one shot past.

"They are shooting from a distance. If they hit you with a bullet, you'll have to cut it out, but it's weak, at the end of its flight," advised Trofim.

"Trofim, is that you?" I asked.

He crawled up to me and covered my mouth with his hand. A couple more bullets struck to the left of us. Then they opened fire with rifles and artillery. You could hear the rattling noises of the guns. A minute, two, three, and we were off again.

Rapid rifle fire opened on the left flank. Over our battalion, flares were sighted. They were blue-green and fell ever so slowly. Klimich told me that only the Austrians had such flares, and we had only useless ones that were water damaged. They shoot and shoot them, but they are of no use.

What is this? My sleeve got caught on the barbed wire! How had this happened? I pulled on the sleeve with all my strength. It wouldn't come off. The gunfire was getting worse. All of a sudden I got a really sharp pain in my stomach. I got nauseous, and I felt a cold sweat on my forehead. I was sweating, but at the same time, I was cold. I shivered, and then I was really hot again. Mama, Valya, Daddy, where are you? I'm going to die right now. I'm going to die and never see you again.

"Sasha? Trofim? Where are you?" Nobody answered me. A shrapnel shell exploded close by. The light from the searchlight quickly swept the field. It hid for a second then appeared again in the direction of our scouts.

Not a sound, what should I do? I touched my cheek with my free hand. It was wet. Was I wounded? Is this blood? It's sweat, of course, it's only sweat, I told myself. Don't be scared, don't be scared. I tried to calm myself. Another shrapnel shell exploded, and it was so close. My head hurt so much it felt like a tub of boiling water was spilled on it. Everything was exploding closer and closer to me. The searchlight beam emerged. It swung left, then right, and then back to the middle again.

"Trofim, where are you?" I whispered.

Silence; I heard a machine gun start its rapid fire. Whatever happens, happens. I pulled on my shirtsleeve that was caught. The barbed wire rattled, but the sleeve remained stuck on those damned barbs.

All of a sudden the simplest solution to the situation came to me. Single-handedly, I pulled off my shirt. I freed myself and crawled a few steps. I was scared of the whistle from the bullets. I was so happy that I freed myself that I forgot the best way to crawl was on your side, as Sasha told me, and I got on all fours and just crawled. Only one thing was on my mind, to get to the trenches, just to get there faster!

"What's up? You're that kid, not Sergey, what do they call you, Zina?" said a voice.

By the way he talked, I recognized Chereshenko.

"Where is Sasha?" I asked.

"Sasha is fine, but why are you crawling on all fours? Do you want to get hit with a bullet? When they hit you in the ass, then maybe you will learn your lesson. When the gunfire dies down a little, Zina, get up and then get back down again, if it starts up again, lie there, when it quiets down, run again," he instructed.

The wind was blowing through my shirt on the barbed wire. My ripped-up sleeve hung there in several pieces. In the dugout, bending over my bag, I pulled out a gray shirt and put it on.

"Where did you go, Zina?" Sasha asked.

"I crawled away from you to Trofim. I turned around, and you were not there. So, I thought you were with Chereshenko. And I thought you wouldn't get lost," I explained.

"Hey, Zina, where is your uniform shirt?" he asked.

"Forget about the army shirt, why did you leave me?" I asked.

"I didn't leave you! I crawled away a little. I thought you were right behind me. Tell me, where is your uniform shirt?" he asked again.

"It's hanging on the wire by the Austrians," I answered.

"Have you gone insane? Why did you leave it there?" he asked.

I told Sasha everything that happened.

He laughed loudly and said: "Oh boy, Zina! Are you going to leave your underpants hanging on their wire next time?"

"You're laughing, but you should be embarrassed," I said.

"All right, all right, I won't tell anyone. Maybe Chereshenko didn't even notice you in the dark. The regiment will not attack, Zina. The scouts on the right flank were sighted. Now their plan can't be carried out," he explained.

Enemy artillery fired on the neighboring trenches of the Twelfth Division all night. The close distance from the Austrian trenches saved our battalion from being fired at, because they were afraid of hitting their own troops.

Either from fear or from dread, or maybe from embarrassment of losing my army shirt, I dug my head into my knees and cried.

)))

"I have the honor of being present!" I reported.

The regimental commander sat on a cot in the dugout. There was a small table, and on it stood a small kerosene lamp. On the wall, made of planks, hung a picture of a boy in a cadet uniform with his hair neatly cut. The cadet was sitting on a chair, but his legs didn't reach the floor. There was a big teakettle on top of a suitcase that stood upright. The little gray-haired colonel reached for the newspaper that was lying on the table. His eyes were tearing like Valya's dog Toby. His mustache, stained with nicotine, was very thin at the ends. The old man smiled and spoke to me.

"Stop standing so straight. Stop pretending. What are you trying to be here? Well, this is how things are, your family is looking for you. They request your return home. Will you go?" he asked.

"No, I'm not going back. I like it here. It's not the same as back there. Everything is new and interesting for me here," I explained.

"Well, it's up to you. I will not force you. You'll run away again anyway, but I think you should realize it's not worth it and go home to your parents. They will either kill you or wound you here. Your parents will never be able to get over that. What is it that you like here? Tell me the truth, I am like your father here. My granddaughter Marina is the same age as you, but she isn't like you at all, she is drawn to the monastery, and my grandson, well, that's his picture up there. He is a cadet, you see. Do you understand that it's really dangerous here?"

"I understand, sir."

"You can call me Stanislav Kazmirovitch."

"Well, Stanislav Kazmirovitch, you have to understand that it's very interesting here, and there is work for me here. I will help the wounded."

"Make it clearer, what is so interesting about this place? As for work, if you want to know, that's your fantasy because, in fact, there is much to be done behind the front lines. You can go to the mobile hospital and be a nurse there."

"Stanislav Kazmirovitch, it's not the same there."

"Speak louder and clearer, I don't hear well."

"You have to understand, I'm the only volunteer here, in the whole division, and it's especially interesting here because the conditions are so good."

"Oh! So you want to flirt here! Aren't you a little too young for that?"

"No, that's not it. I just like being the only woman for a whole ten versts."

"Make sure this amusement of yours doesn't cost you too heavily," he warned.

"So what if I am a girl? Girls can fight in the war, and they can march too. At first it's a little hard, but, for example, I managed, and I even got stronger, and I know how to shoot."

"Did you kill a lot of Austrians?"

"No, I didn't shoot at them yet."

"Who did you shoot at?"

"The jackdaws."

"Oh, you, soldiers don't shoot at birds. All right then, go. Here take this," he said and gave me a chocolate bar.

"Semen, show the lady to her company," the colonel ordered.

The servant politely showed me the way. We walked out of the commander's dugout.

"All right, Semen, you can go back now, I know the way myself. I am a soldier just like you," I said. I stood on my tiptoes and patted him on the shoulder, saying, "Go, go."

"You are a soldier, well isn't that a wonder," he said. Semen, disobeying the regimental commander, turned and quietly crept to his dugout.

)))

A visiting scout and Trofim were very involved in a card game.

"Zina, tomorrow we are going to make a new dugout. This one is getting too small. You have a shovel, but you have no rifle. I asked the platoon leader, but he won't give us any. There aren't enough rifles. He promised to get a revolver for you," Trofim said.

I took my place on a cot and went to sleep.

"Zina is sleeping, and it's rough to live with her. Ever since I found out she's a girl, I can't sleep. I don't have any peace. I can't stay with her under one roof anymore. I thought about getting together with her, but she's too young, she might whine and cause problems," Sasha explained.

"Oh, stop it, Sasha, you are a person with no patience," Trofim remarked.

"Yeah, maybe, Trofim, but Zina just looks so good," Sasha added.

I lay there under the blanket, everything was such a blur. Then I fell asleep.

)))

I woke up early. I felt a knot inside my stomach, and I felt horribly, and it's all because there were all kinds of obstacles in my path. If I went outside under the open sky with no door or anything, danger was all around me. There was no way you could feel safe. I rolled my head from front to back, side to side. I was always on my guard, on the lookout if any of the men were coming, and if they were, how close they were, either that or if there was a shell exploding nearby.

I wrote a letter home:

Dearest Mother, Father and Valya,

I beg you not to worry about me and to stop trying to get me to come home. I'm not leaving from here. I had to endure a lot of struggles before I could get to the front lines. After I left Kazan on a wagon stuffed with people on their way to war, I successfully made it to the Brody station, and I was held up there to be sent back on the prison train. I got a chance to run and soon enough made it to the regiment.

At first I hid the fact that I was a girl, but then I got tired of playing the role of a stupid boy and told everybody the truth. Dearest mother, send me some underclothes, sew some male garments, it's more comfortable for me, and send me male underpants immediately. Make them short. And send me some stockings. They gave me a uniform, and I resewed it to fit my height. Valya, send me cigarettes, as much as you can. I have a friend, a soldier, he received a package from home and treated me to gingerbread cookies. He is a great guy and recently I saw how he got beat up by an officer and that same officer called me a "pup," but when my disguise was uncovered he sent me chocolate. My good and dear ones, don't worry about me, there are plenty of people here. I am not the only one. One of the other scouts promised to send this letter for me. He is going to Kiev, and his eyes hurt terribly. Many kisses.

Zina

CHAPTER 4

Zina's division moves to a new position to attack the village of
Zalischyky and the railway station at the nearby village of Okna in
southeastern Galicia. Zina participates in the successful attack on
Austrian and German positions defending the Okna railway station,
and after the battle her unit relocates to the nearby village of Dzhany.

The young forest was wild with summer happiness. The soldiers
arranged themselves in a bivouac. Sasha looked at the swaying birch
tree, there was a bluebird rocking on it. She was pecking at the stomach of a white moth. He commented, "She is eating. Look at her. She's
about the size of that moth herself. She's a lucky one! She's free."

"The forest is so fragrant, and there are lots of flowers. My Mashka
loves flowers. Here take some. Behind our village we have an abun-
dance of blackberries," Trofim added.

I looked at Trofim's present, at the purple bells. I listened to Sasha
and Trofim. Their voices got soft. They spoke with a gentle fondness
of birds of the forest and of flowers. Somewhere a gun fired.

By morning walking about two versts through the woods, our battalion reached the village of Mikhalka, on the border of the forest.[1]
After spending two hours there, we walked another fifteen versts. The
regiment stopped, and we started to prepare for the night's rest. The
soldiers lined up their rifles and set up the tents.

After drinking tea, we sat around the fire and roasted potatoes
over soot. Trofim's whole cheek was swollen again. He took Klim-

ich's tobacco pouch and filling it with hot soot, pressed it against his cheek. Walking up to us, one of Trofim's countrymen joined us and said:

"I came to check up on you. I have news. Today I heard that they are taking our commander away from us. I heard it myself. He told Lieutenant Colonel Krivdin: 'The officers offend me, they say I give the soldiers all kinds of indulgences, and now they behave inappropriately.' It will be sad if they take away Svirskovo. God forbid they send someone like Plakhov from the Kybansky Regiment. We'll all lose our teeth. Maybe they'll give us someone like Balme. Today I saw his servant. Boy, does he have funny stories about him. He told me: 'Right before Balme goes to sleep, he asks me, Ocip, where is my colonel's insignia?' He gives it to him, and Balme puts it under his pillow and goes to sleep. In the morning he wakes up and asks, 'Ocip, am I the colonel?' He tells him that's right, you are the lieutenant colonel. Then he screams, 'I'm no lieutenant colonel, you son of a bitch, I am the colonel!' And the next night, it happens all over again. He says he's sick of him. He would be happier if they just give him all the colonel's insignia he wants, so he would just shut up."

After Trofim's countryman finished his story, he said, "All right, guys, that's all the news I have. What do you have for me, Trofim?"

"Well, Zina got a package. She got cigarettes from home. You're not the only one with news. Krivdin made Chereshenko his servant. There they stand together," Trofim pointed.

Skinny, dark, short, like something that buzzes, Lieutenant Colonel Krivdin, the Fourth Battalion's commander, stood next to his new servant, whose height was to be envied, and spoke compulsively. He took small rapid steps walking around Chereshenko. Then he would stop, it seemed, as if he would jump around next to him and scream something indecipherable. Apparently this new servant wasn't to his taste. A group of soldiers was gathering not too far away from them.

"Be quiet, guys, what happened over there?" someone asked.

Leaping to Chereshenko, Krivdin did another little jump, and we heard his high-pitched voice: "Bend down here, you son of a bitch, bend down, damn Ukrainian, you stupid ass, bend down here!" And swinging his arms, Krivdin started jumping again. Chereshenko, as if to tease the lieutenant colonel, raised his head even higher. After a few more jumps, Krivdin just sat down in the hay, pulled out a handkerchief, wiped his forehead, and fanned himself, and then from exhaustion, just let his head fall on his shoulder.

"He wanted to hit him. He wanted to smack him, but Chereshenko didn't give in," said Trofim, forgetting about his toothache and bursting into laughter. We all laughed and were certain that as soon as tomorrow Chereshenko would be sent back to us.

)))

I spent a week resting. I showered, cleaned myself and relaxed. I came back to the regiment, which was posted in the reserve lines. Trofim's countryman told us the latest news in the morning; the regiments will lead an attack on Zalischyky and the Okna train station, and the cavalry will follow up on the enemy.[2]

Before sunrise they pulled our battalion into the forest. There in a big ravine, Tekintsi cavalrymen made themselves at home.[3] They wore sheepskin hats with gloomy bronze faces and would check on their horses every other minute. I had never seen such lean horses before. They had small heads, white manes, and long gray tails. The cavalrymen started a fire. There was a bloody white duck quivering on a curved sword. It began to smell really bad, and the smell burned your eyes. An infantry officer gave an order to put out the fire. A cavalryman smiled and answered: "Why do you fight unfairly? Why do you hide in your trenches?"

The fires burned. A warning round was fired. The whole cavalry rushed to put out the fires. But it's easier to put a fire out than to scatter the smoke. Shrapnel shells exploding over the forest were replaced by high explosive shells. The cavalrymen ran to their horses in the chaos. A shell exploded making a huge cloud of smoke. A shell fragment wounded a horse, and the cavalryman bent over it. The beautiful horse stretched out its long legs on the fresh grass now covered in warm blood. Struggling to pick up its head, with a dimming gaze, the horse stared at its ripped-open stomach. It wheezed in agony. One of the cavalrymen hurriedly threw down his coat, and with the help of the rest, placed the horse on it. The Tekintsi pulled along the heavy weight of their war companion under the intense artillery fire. By evening the artillery fire ceased, but not the whining. The forest turned pink from the sunset. Bent over the corpse of his horse, the wide-eyed Tekintsi cavalryman quietly cried over his loss in silence.

)))

From the morning on, the orderlies hurried through the dugouts and the communications trenches. The field telephone buzzed like a bee, calling officers to the regimental commander. The worried faces and hurried steps of the officers made the soldiers tense. Thoughts of war weighed heavily on our minds, just like the Austrian hilltop positions that overlooked the Russian trenches. Orders arrived from the division headquarters to advance our positions. Junior officers told the soldiers about the oncoming attack, adding: "We have to take the enemy's position, General Mitchvolodov gave the order." The soldiers silently prepared for the fight.

At night the field kitchens came, and the officers' servants were like a line of ducklings lined up with their aluminum bowls clattering. The soldiers ate without appetites. After eating, they all gathered, and sitting on the ground, they began falling asleep while leaning on their rifles.

At sunrise the batteries began firing. Clouds of explosions covered the whole field of Austro-German trenches. They were silent. Somewhere from the right came an electric shock hitting our tense nerves, and the call, "Forward!"

The junior officers, in their gray overcoats, hurriedly jumping out of the trenches, ran ten paces or so and immediately got down. The soldiers, unsure and cautious, raised their heads, got up, and then got down on the ground in a disorderly line. The Austrians didn't open fire. The line of soldiers got up and walked forward. Following them emerged another line of gray overcoats. The enemy started to fire weakly, but the first line of men didn't get down. Only certain soldiers carrying machine guns stopped to shoot at the path ahead of them to clear the way for soldiers behind them. There were only about six hundred to seven hundred paces left to the first enemy trenches. The officers stopped to give commands. The soldiers started running in groups from one mound of ground to the next.

At this time the Austro-German soldiers, aligned in a horseshoe, came alive. The calm fire of the German guns pinned us to the ground. The artillery fire was directly hitting our trenches. The second line, walking bravely behind the cover of the first, got distended and buried themselves in the ground. Frequent gunfire; the machine guns started to fire. The enemy didn't account for this, the German artillery couldn't fire on the oncoming troops because they were afraid of hitting their own men. There was a howl of "Hooray!" The wide gateway of the barbed wire, cut at night, served its purpose. The Austrians ran around like ants. In their panic, they ran out of their trenches.

"Get him, get him!" yelled the officers.

"Stab him, stab him!" the soldiers yelled.

Soldiers ran along the communications trench. Their attention was fixed on the Austrian satchels.

"Look, guys, they have Krones, oh my, Krones!"[4]

"Don't get held up! Forward!" an officer shouted.

Lying in a communications trench was a wounded Austrian with his legs stretched out. Blood poured out of his fat stomach. Without even jumping over him, soldiers stepped on him with their heavy boots that crushed his chest. With an inhuman sound escaping him, the Austrian picked up his head slightly and begged, "Shoot me!"

Trying my hardest, I dragged the wounded man to a dugout and climbed back up. At that moment the Austrians, without even reaching their reserve trenches, counterattacked. Our batteries opened fire. Everything was mixed up. The enemy rows of soldiers fell perfectly aligned. But they continued to walk forward, and behind them was a line of Germans. Our soldiers were afraid to move; to everyone it seemed as if the enemy could see only them among the whole mass of soldiers. The shells were hitting our own men. People were dropping; the ground was covered in blood. Throwing his arms up, Lieutenant Yerosh fell wounded right next to me. But the heads turned, and we saw far left where the Sevastopolsky Regiment was attacking, and the Austrians were running from their reserve lines. People ran all over. The soldiers got up and without command went forward. With screams, whistles, and the glistening of swords, a group of cavalry approached, sweeping everything in their path. The Austrian line was shattered, and everyone went in all different directions. A machine gun began to fire but then ceased. Throwing their rifles down, the Austrians, with raised arms yelled, "We surrender!" as they walked toward our soldiers. The German line froze in its tracks.

Like the wind, the cavalry rushed past us on the right. The Tekintsi, in their black sheepskin hats, leaned close to the white manes of their horses. They wore grim expressions of an unhappy fate as they galloped forward.

The Okna station was conquered. Along with it, its trains with Austrian soldiers in fresh uniforms. To their great dismay, the Austrians were no longer able to give any orders.

After the battle, the officers of the battalion opened some metal containers of the Austrians and treated themselves to rum. The soldiers, taking off their dirty underclothes, put on thin, fresh, clean, Austrian undergarments. I walked around examining the enemy's dugouts. Everything was so nice in there, but the Germans, they seemed so scary in these dark caves! Now when I saw them up close, they seemed merciless and cruel, but at the same time I had a feeling of such great respect for them.

I saw Trofim. The butt of his rifle was decorated in bloody designs. He sat there wrapping what was left of his gauze bandage. A pigeon sat on his knee with its red feet bent. Trofim carefully bandaged its wounded wing. Hiding the gauze, Trofim petted the pigeon's head with his forefinger. The pigeon slept.

Sasha, sitting on a pile of empty cans, looked through an Austrian knapsack, and shifting his cap to the side and twisting his hair, couldn't take his eyes off a picture of a happy Austrian girl staring back at him.

Before sunrise we left the dugouts, and after two more stops we came to the village of Dzhany. I was walking to my room and ran into David Markovitch. His black, curly hair, wide forehead, big, gray eyes, straight nose, puffy lips with a sweet smile, made his face quite attractive. He stopped me, and we started talking.

"Tell me, David Markovitch, didn't they call you Shansky? We were on an assignment together, do you remember?" I asked.

"Yes, that's me. So, Zina, are you planning to be in the army for much longer?" he inquired.

"Yes. I'm going to stay here forever. It's interesting," I replied.

"Interesting?" Markovitch stared at me and smiled, but that smile wasn't genuine, and I got uncomfortable.

"There isn't too much that's interesting here. Of course for you it's interesting here. You are our only one. Everyone spoils you. You don't notice all of our problems or maybe you try not to see them. You are way too preoccupied with yourself," he commented.

"Why do you think that? Didn't you see how I dragged a wounded enemy soldier to the side?"

"A German?" he asked.

"No, an Austrian," I said.

"It's all the same. If you distinguish yourself, you too can get a medal. They will write about you in the newspapers, and then you will really like it here. It's all empty, Zina, and because you're so young, you don't understand this. Let's get acquainted better. Come visit me. I'm staying in that house over there. Will you come?"

"We're not about to go anywhere? No? Well, then sure I'll come. Will you teach me how to read a map? Do you know field maps well?" I asked.

"Yes. I will teach you," he replied.

Parting with him, I was on my way to my landlady. I got to sleep alone due to the commander's orders, but sometimes they make me room with Sasha or Trofim.

What's this? Where were these new small boots from? There was a note:

Zina,

I had these made for you. And they are making a jacket to fit you too. I am taking on the role of your guardian. I am at the house of the Roman Catholic priest, come visit. We have strawberry jam.

Zambor

I tried on the boots several times. They were nice. They were a good fit, but I took them off and threw them in a corner. After a minute I put them on again. They are perfect for marches. My big boots gave me blisters and forced me to travel in the field kitchen wagons. The field kitchens clank so loudly, and during breaks the soldiers would come and make fun of me, saying, "So, Zina, you signed up to be in the weak group? As soon as they found out you were a girl, they put you right onto the wagon, and you ride around like a princess!"

I'll take the boots; I can, but I won't go to the lieutenant. So what if they have strawberry jam. Zambor is mean and makes me uncomfortable.

I put on Zambor's present and went for a walk. I stopped near the aid station. The wounded soldiers sat near the hut. They were impatiently waiting to be sent to the rear.

"Are we going to be tormented much longer? When are they going to send us to the hospital? It's nauseating here. They are testing our patience, and the wounded can't get any peace. What are we suffering for? My father wrote me from home. This is the third month he is going into town for help with no results. There are three of us brothers, and we were all sent to war. Father is old, he can't work," a soldier complained.

"It would be nice to go home, brothers. I would rather irritate my wounds with kerosene than go back to the front lines. On my holy cross, I won't. Who needs this war?" commented another.

The soldiers looked askance at me. These looks stung me, and for some reason I became very aggravated. That was the same way Markovitch looked at me and smiled.

I returned to my hut. My landlady came in.

"Grandma, boil ten eggs for me," I told her.

"What do you need so many for? You are little, you don't need so many. Do you have any money?" she asked.

"Not right now, but I will pay you back tomorrow," I said.

"Forget you soldiers with your promises of tomorrow. You'll leave at night. No, you can't pay me back tomorrow. I can keep after you soldiers for a long time. Come on, get out of here, the young children want to see you," she said.

"Grandma, you are mean," I replied.

"I am not mean, no. I cannot feed all of you. Those over there in the furry hats, they took a good goose from the Vivtorek family. I won't give it to you. Look at this brave one over here," she said. The old lady slammed the door, walking out onto the porch. Outside a bunch of kids surrounded me.

"Priska, hey, Priska, look at this one. Her boots are like that of a Russian," said one of the children. The kids surrounded me from all sides. They were touching me and examining me. The old lady came out on the doorstep and told them all to go to bed.

"I will go to war too," said a black-eyed little boy who smiled at me.

I thought, what if I met a kid like this in battle? I wouldn't shoot at him.

In the moonlight, the cottages looked even whiter than in the daytime. There were three in a row. They looked like white mushrooms. Behind them was a big cottage covered in thin metal, two more little ones, and in that fenced cottage lived David Markovitch.

"I am here, hello. Is it too late?" I asked.

"Good day, Zina. Where did you get those boots?" he asked.

"Here," I gave Markovitch the note Zambor left me.

"Strawberry jam. Well, that's not bad. But I don't advise you to go to the lieutenant. I don't have jam, but I do have honey," he said.

Markovitch began to smoke and pace the room, at times pausing by me, observing. I looked at the map that was on the table, and I asked him how to decipher orientation signs. He explained it quite thoroughly.

"All right, Zina, that's enough for today, let's talk about something. Now tell me, do you like it here?" he asked.

"Yes, it's interesting," I said.

"It's pretty original of you to find it interesting in the place where death resides, where a war machine destroys human bodies in the interests of the rich men. Don't you ever wonder who needs this war, and why young healthy Germans and Austrians who are being destroyed by this war suddenly became our enemies? I guess I understand you.

You are young, and there are things you learn only with experience. But make sure you don't turn out to be the case where seven nannies watch a child missing an eye," he said.

"I don't understand you at all, David Markovitch, who are my nannies?" I asked.

"Oh stop it seriously! You don't even notice how the officers babysit you. Sometimes I look into the officers' store and on more than one occasion I've seen the officers' servants buying you candy and perfume and other things. Everyone tries to make you happy in some way to get your attention. You are a big tease for everyone here. Even in the face of death, they still want you, it's so obvious," he replied.

"I am not friendly with many officers, and I don't pay any special attention to anyone," I said.

"The fact that you don't pay any special attention to anyone, I've noticed myself, but what I am talking about here is your insensitivity to everyone's feelings. I was walking behind you one day, and I saw a soldier ask you for a cigarette, and you refused to give it to him," he said.

"David Markovitch, those cigarettes weren't mine, the battalion commander asked me to buy them for him," I answered.

"Whether they were yours or not is completely irrelevant, you know if you took ten of them, our lovely battalion commander wouldn't say anything, only smile. I already told you that you don't notice anything around. Do you even know that this horrible war we are fighting in, the same war you find amusement in, doesn't even make sense? This is a horrible war; it's terrible in its senselessness. The rich, Zina, they are forcing people to go to war and by doing this, they are ruining the already sad lands of the peasants. And what does this homeland and government give the peasants? A beating and lack of culture. The capitalists make us go to war. They make people poor with their ridiculous taxes, and the people that don't have anything to begin with! Do you know that this whole war is a terrible lie? There is a fog that dawns over the people, they don't see, and the fog is coming this way, convincing the people they need to protect their country and their czar. But soon the people will put the pieces together and realize who their real enemy is. Time doesn't stop, life goes by, and it teaches people.

You're living, right, Zina? Well life, Zina, is the people itself, and you need to understand people. Are you really that inattentive? Do you know that for Zambor, the squire's son, all these people are nothing but little tin soldiers? You say it's amusing, interesting, think about these words, you are not a spoiled little child anymore, Zina, you're sixteen. Here people learn about each other even more, and you won't leave here the same person, Zina, war changes you. I would like to see you and speak with you in a year, a year at war is a long year. Don't close up inside yourself like a snail, open your heart and give the people everything good and wonderful inside of it. Don't pretend, and for God's sake, stop your unnecessary flirting," he said. Markovitch took a break, and his face turned red, while his eyes wearily, angrily darted from the window to the door.

My soul ached from this unpleasant conversation with David Markovitch.

"David Markovitch, I'm going to go," I said.

"Why, are you sick of me already? Are you bored listening to me?" he asked.

"No, not bored, it's just too much. I'm going to go," I said.

Somebody knocked at the door. Sasha walked in. David Markovitch gave Sasha some milk and honey. I was so sleepy and covering myself with the blanket on Markovitch's bed, I fell asleep. I don't know how long I slept, but when I opened my eyes, I didn't want to move and lay there facing the wall. David and Sasha spoke, whispering.

"And that's how things are, Gusev, so how do you like Zina?" asked David.

"Eh, so-so," replied Sasha.

"Sasha, you are shameless! Why am I just so-so?" I said.

"You little . . . ! Why did you lie there silent for an hour, but when we start talking about you, then you speak up?" Sasha asked.

"Sasha, don't be mean!" I said.

"Stop squealing!" he said.

"I am not squealing! Stop fighting with me! Shameless! I have a conscience, why are you being so nosy?" I said.

"I'm not nosy! Shut up!" he said.

"Oh stop it, both of you. Leave her alone. Sasha, why did you attack her? It wasn't some big conspiracy, so what if she heard us!" David said.

"It's not about a conspiracy, it's about having a conscience!" replied Sasha.

"That's enough, make up right now, both of you!" said David.

I was holding back laughter. Looking at Sasha, I stretched out my hand, and he slapped it hard and squeezed it. We bid our farewells and left.

)))

I went in the direction of the house I was staying at. The whole village slept. The sounds of artillery in the distance didn't disturb the peace. My landlady's yard had a fence around it made of tree branches woven together. Creaking, the wicket-door let me in. On the front porch there was a cat. Woken up by the noise, it got up and stretched. Meowing, it rubbed itself against my boots. I knocked on the door, and the old lady unhappily opened the door, letting the cat and me in.

"You little devil, out at night," she said and went over to her half of the room.

In the gardens, the poplars stood tall. The village was filled with the aroma of ripe apples. The limb, on which a pear hung, leaned on a wicker fence. The fallen pears were swarming with bees that love something sweet. The rosy-cheeked, dark-eyed Yana, my landlady's daughter, helped her mother gather apples. With her sharp teeth, she bit into a juicy apple. There was a flashing red handkerchief amongst the trees. The five-year-old granddaughter, Priska, carried dried branches into the little house where they were burned, throwing them into the fire. Yana stopped and looked at the top of the apple tree. It wasn't a big tree, but there was only one apple on it.

I saw how an officer jumped over the fence, it was Lieutenant Zambor. Swinging a stick, he walked toward Yana. He walked up to the tree with one apple. He threw his stick up into the tree. Leaves fell. Yana jumped up.

"Don't touch it. What do you need it for? Don't you see there is only one? Let it hang there, don't touch it. You hear me?" she said.

"Stupid girl, what do you need it for when you are so juicy yourself?" he replied. In one swift movement, Zambor grabbed her waist. She tried to free herself from his embrace. Her bright-colored scarf fell at her feet.

"Oh God, oh no!" screamed Yana, so it was heard throughout the whole garden. Grandma ran to her, leaning on a walking stick.

"I salute you, your Excellency!" I said, after running up to them.

The lieutenant jumped away from the girl and, looking at me with his cold glassy eyes, picked up his stick and walked away.

Yana looked at me with blurred vision. The look on her face was one of gratitude. She leaned on the apple tree and quietly cried.

CHAPTER 5

Zina's regiment repulses a fierce German attack on July 5, 1916.
After the battle, she and several of her comrades begin discussing
their growing discontentment with the war. It is unclear whether
Dubinskaya is using the Gregorian calendar or the Julian calendar,
which would make the date June 23.

Part of the First Battalion's area at Dzhany was regarded as very important for some reason. The officers referred to it as the "key position" in
conversations with each other. The companies took up positions at the
graveyard and windmill, which stood at the edge of the village. From
the windmill to the end of the graveyard, there flowed a narrow and
smelly river. The water was only about knee-deep, but impossible to
get through. It was bright green, as if it had been painted, and along
the river a few flowers bloomed.

The graveyard was in a dry patch, and its abandoned part stretched
upward toward the village where there were gentle birch trees and
shrubs growing. From this point to the right, for about ten versts, you
could see the trenches, and to the left about 100 feet away was the
windmill. There was a dam by the mill, and the little man-made pond
looked like a bowl filled with water. There was no one in the mill, and
the millstones grinded against each other for no useful reason. The
peasants tried to get permission to stop the turning wheel, but were
rejected every single time by an officer.

German trenches and their batteries were visible from the graveyard. I couldn't tell whether they were real or fake, but at sunrise I could see their artillery was different from ours. Two of our companies took up positions at the graveyard; one took up position at the mill, and one was in the reserve at the edge of the forest. The whole graveyard was filled with trenches. Every day they would get deeper and deeper to store supplies, and the gun port openings were being reinforced with a new layer of dirt. For a while the peasants requested permission from Lieutenant Colonel Krivdin to collect the skeletons. He didn't allow it. As soon as Captain Krapivansky allowed the peasants in the First Battalion's area to gather the skeletons, they dug a mass grave for those thrown out of their last havens near the village and put all of the remains inside.

At night an allocation of villagers worked on building timber barriers and strengthening the barbed wire defenses. Five rows of barriers rose before the graveyard. They dug the ground by the mill too, but there wasn't much progress or hard work there.

The valley was calm. During the day when the sun shone its brightest, there were big dark-colored butterflies fluttering above the yellow flowers, and at night guards protected the pathways.

The past few days the Germans remained quiet. Before there wasn't a day the Germans didn't attack. No one even thought of attacking them, but just in case we had to run, we counted how many versts we could do in a day.

Every day during the week, at sunrise, noon, and at sunset, when the German barbed wire was visible, they sent us their "mail," as Sasha called it, when the bullets came our way.

)))

Above the graveyard, high in the sky, a shrapnel shell exploded, and small lead balls lashed at the old crosses. Two shrapnel and five high-explosive shells were the appointed ration. During this time all activity in the trenches ceased. The soldiers flattened themselves against the trench walls, and the officers on duty focused on their trench periscopes.

"The Germans, they are a very precise people, they won't miss," said Trofim, as soon as the first shrapnel shell exploded above the trenches.

"They're always right on point," confirmed Sasha, squinting his blue eyes and carelessly walking through the trenches.

Krivdin, like a turtle, peeked out from his dugout, and after going back in soon emerged again. Not even glancing at the trenches, he looked questioningly at the artilleryman on duty. He appraised the situation by the arc of the officer's back. Then, without saying anything, he got back into his dugout.

This went on for seven long days. During the day, you could see the anxiety. When the Germans would cease firing, normal life would resume in the trenches.

The soldiers of our company would leave with the sergeant and noncommissioned officers to put up barbed wire and dig our trenches. The officers gathered in Krivdin's bunker and spent all day there. At night a third of the soldiers kept watch on guard duty. They weren't allowed to sit or lie down. They stood at the gun ports. At the sign of any movement Krivdin would jump out of his bunker and would listen, placing his hand to his ear. The field telephone was in use all night. Krivdin would call the commander of the reserve company several times to make sure he didn't go to sleep. The unexpectedness of the night attacks scared everyone.

At sunrise on July 5, the Germans sent their "first mail." Counting out two shrapnel and five shells, people began to unglue themselves from the walls. The commissary men began carrying buckets of tea through the communications trenches.

"It would be nice to drink something warm for the insides," Trofim lazily remarked, as he took out an aluminum spoon without a handle.

Zhhhhhh . . . vaxx . . .—there was a loud sound in the communications trench; above Trofim the dirt roof broke. A bucket with a piece of a commissary man's arm, disconnected at the elbow, attached to the handle, rolled toward his feet, spilling what was left of the murky water. After that explosion, ten, maybe twenty, or even thirty followed.

In front of the graveyard and the dam there were eruptions of fire and soil. Officers piled out of Krivdin's bunker, securing their swords as they ran. Krivdin was with them, and he looked blacker than ever; the color of his face was blending in with his brown uniform coat. Crouching, he ran through the communications trench, stopped at one of the gun ports, and a second later, jumped over to the periscope.

"They are firing without a break," Trofim commented.

"They are firing a week's worth of ammunition in advance," added the pointy-nosed Bashmakin, who recently returned from the infirmary.

"We burst their bubble, and this is what comes out," joked Sasha.

"Why don't you go fix it?" Trofim told Sasha.

"Go peek out, maybe you will make it," snarled Sasha. "Serve the world, brother; look at what has happened to our people."

The Germans fired as if there were a row of hundreds of giants out there. The artillery tore the ground to shreds. Pieces of blown-up crosses were flying into the trenches.

"Officers, take your positions. We have to wait for the attack," came word.

Our artillery was silent. The battery commander was busy with Krivdin and kept sending messages to his battery over the phone. The Germans didn't stop firing. The rounds began to crack in front of the graveyard, where the barbed wire was. Bashmakin stood by the gun port and shook his head. His chin stretched forward and looked as if it were going to come off.

"This fire, this fire, ripping everything to shreds! They're shaving us to pieces, the sons of bitches. There isn't a thread left," murmured Bashmakin, as he shook his head.

I pushed Bashmakin and stood by the gun port myself. The German trenches looked lifeless. Then I saw a couple of figures emerge. They crawled up to their barbed wire and took down the barriers. In front of me, where just a half hour ago stood our own barrier, now was a freshly cleared space, with the exception of a few pieces of timber here and there.

The German shells continued to fly over our trenches. The ground by the mill was now exploding. All of a sudden something popped, and the man-made lake lashed out, falling in loud cascades over the whole dam. There was a large white mass of fizzing foam. The wheel in the mill stopped turning. Artillery continued to fall on the trenches and near them. The artillery officer gave his battery commands. You could hear solitary firing from their side, and then the cannons began firing nonstop and were really loud. Lines of Germans came out of the trenches and moved through the ripe rye field. They moved forward. The machine guns began to fire. Dead and wounded Germans covered the field, but their lines began to separate, and they continued to move forward in groups. The German reserves kept coming, and as if they never had any losses, they continued on toward our lines. Our soldiers didn't move from the gun ports and continued to fire at the Germans.

The roar of the enemy's guns was never ending. The Third Platoon of our company, leaving half its soldiers in the trenches, moved to the reserve lines. The Germans got closer and closer. All of a sudden there was a command from an officer, "We're going to counterattack!"

The company commander, Lieutenant Yerosh, unbuckling his sword, grabbed the first rifle he saw from a dead soldier and started climbing up the trench steps.[1] The soldiers followed him, one after the other. The Second Company was crawling out of the nearby trenches. In about two minutes the whole division was out of the trenches. The reserve soldiers came from the village. Lieutenant Zambor came with them. He ran around screaming, "God bless you! Go forth, brothers!" The reserves marched forward, Zambor stayed behind with Krivdin.

The German artillery started reaching our lines. Men were already down; they were falling on the growing rye. The soldiers kept moving.

About a hundred steps away from the Germans, Lieutenant Yerosh yelled hooray and went on to attack the Germans. The soldiers didn't fall behind either. Shouts of hooray were heard all over the rye field.

The Germans hesitated, but in half a minute they ran towards the Russian lines. In one second the swords were crossed. Their artillery fire was directed towards our reserves. From the Russian lines sounds of "ugh" and "hooray" were heard. The enemy fought in silence. Our soldiers fought, making as much noise as if they were chopping down trees. The Germans fought with careful, thought-out moves. Their faces looked blue under their black helmets.

Some big soldier stabbed one of ours, who seemed like a child before the giant; his eyes were fixed on the point of the enemy's bayonet. He dropped his gun and with trembling hands grabbed onto the bayonet. Falling on the ground with a hole in his stomach, he tried to tighten all his muscles as if to stop the steel from going through his stomach.

The Russians and the Germans fought with all their might. In the distance both our reserves and the German reserves stopped. Looking each other in the face, both the Russian and German soldiers backed away.

Both reserves went back into their trenches. For a long time, step by step watching each other, they held on tightly to their guns and moved back. At this time the artillery fire died down.

)))

It seemed as if the river were evaporating with the hot July sun. Covered in moss, the mill was completely silent. Gusts of wind would make the rye in the fields swish back and forth like the tide, as if they were calling someone.

The storm of bullets ruined the crops. With any gust of wind, the air smelled of dead bodies. People started to hide their faces in their shirts. The smell was seeping into everything. The air was poisoned. Trofim used a shovel to dig heaps of soil. He fell to the ground smelling the fresh soil and breathing in its aroma. The soldiers wanted to drink. They gravitated towards the buckets, and holding their noses, they drank the water that had been tainted by the dead. These were torturous days.

At noon there was a group of officers headed toward us from the German trenches. They walked with a white flag. Two of our officers were sent out to meet them. They tied a handkerchief to the German lieutenant's eyes and led him to our dugouts. Zambor spoke with the German. Both sides were agreeing to remove the corpses.

I walked next to a morose artillery soldier—Ivanov. There was a patch of land where German and Russian bodies lay. Among the rye, the polish on the helmets of the Germans shined in the light on their beastly heads. The eyes of one German soldier popped out of his head. The brown-bubbled skin popped near his ear. The pus that was leaking out was held up by the giant flies stuck in it. Flies with green bellies slowly crawled out of the soldier's widely opened mouth. Right by him there was a Russian soldier, flat out on the ground. More than half of his skull was blown off, and in the huge gash flesh-eating bugs were moving. The palms of the dead soldier were turned upward.

In the golden rye field, Lieutenant Yerosh lay dead, his arm seeping with pus, still holding onto his rifle. A big bug with whiskers was eating away at a cigarette case lying by his feet. In the afternoon heat there was not one small gust of wind. At times it felt like you stopped breathing.

"It's horrible what their bodies have been reduced to," said the male nurse Nayumich, horrified. He crossed his chest. The nurses quickly dug a hole. There was a terrible stench in the air again from contact with the corpses, which had pus seeping out of them.

"Guys, my insides are turning, I'm going to throw up," a nurse complained, as he walked over to the side and threw up.

The gloomy Ivanov cursed everyone and then quietly uttered, "Those who started this should see it; it should be shoved in their faces! Rascals!"

"Who are you scolding?" I asked.

"What do you need to know for, you volunteering idiot?" he replied.

Ivanov maliciously smirked and walked away. The July afternoon became very hot and stuffy like never before. I was afraid. Ivanov's words scared me.

They are burying the dead. The regimental priest diligently waved his thurible, and the sweet smell of incense mixed with the smell of the bodies was nauseating. The dead were covered with soil. Insects circled above the graves.

Nighttime. I had nightmares. It's as if I've become a dog, and the only thing that's mine is my head. Wagging my tail, I run through the swollen corpses. I lick the pus by my ear. The pus seeps through my nose, into my throat, choking me.

I woke up in a cold sweat. I'm scared. It's quiet in the dugout. I put my hand over my wide-open mouth. My throat was dry. I couldn't breathe well, and now I couldn't sleep.

Those wounded that could walk were on their way to the aid station. Artilleryman Kirilov, struggling, walked through the trench holding his right hand.

"I wish we would hurry out of here," he said, writhing with pain. He quickened his step. His bloody uniform was falling off his shoulders.

"I hope it doesn't get me again," he repeated, and falling and tripping over himself, he hurried out of the trenches. Not too far away from him, a shrapnel shell exploded.

The new regimental commander, Colonel Plakhov, stuffed his pipe with tobacco. The wounded artilleryman walked passed him.

"Stop, you son of a bitch!" shouted the colonel.

Sergeant Dybelo, a military policeman, hearing the voice of his master, magically appeared immediately right before him.

"Stop him!" shouted Plakhov, pointing at the slowly moving artilleryman and blowing smoke rings. The wounded Kirilov was stopped. With his hands behind his back, the regimental commander walked towards him.

"Why did you graze me when you walked past me and not apologize?" he asked.

Instinctively, the soldier's left arm held his wounded right shoulder.

"Answer me, you son of a bitch!" demanded the colonel.

"I am wounded, and I am going to get my shoulder bandaged," Kirilov said.

"You don't respect those higher up," replied the colonel. Plakhov hit him with a stick.

"Spare me, just spare me, your Excellen . . ."—the soldier didn't even finish, he fainted. His arm that was so carefully held in place hit the ground. We picked up Kirilov. He regained consciousness.

"It doesn't matter anymore. I just want to go home faster. And when I am there, I will tell everyone, so they will know what we fight for. David Markovitch was right when he said we should fight for our land and our peasant interests. Down with those cruel people. Why do they have to torture me?" Kirilov questioned.

"He wasn't even ashamed to hurt the wounded," confirmed the male nurse.

"So how are you? Are you able to go? Because we can carry you on the stretchers. There they are. Come on, Zina, help us a little," the nurse said.

"It hurts. It feels like my bone is being scraped," answered Kirilov. We carried him.

"You got strong, Zina, when you got here you were feeble and so frail. We thought if the wind blew, you would fall, but look at you now," the nurse commented.

I was warmed by the gentle smile of the nurse and Kirilov.

)))

In these July days of endless fighting, nobody smiled. Markovitch, Sasha, Ivanov, and I met up pretty often. Ivanov would look at me moodily during our marches, twice we were side by side in battle, and yesterday he said to me, "Maybe you are right, maybe a girl can fight."

"Tell me that's not right, Ivanov," I answered.

"If it's necessary, my Nactya will leave the factory and come here too. You got that?" he added forcefully.

But I didn't understand why his last words sounded so mean and strict. After every conversation with Ivanov I was so mad at myself— why didn't I speak to him as I did to the other soldiers, but instead used some kind of subservient tone. Maybe because I wanted his trust? I wanted him to consider me an equal. But not with my valor in battle, not my patience in the trenches, not with my endurance during the marches could I gain his trust.

)))

Four soldiers sat on a bench in our dugout, and two tried to find a spot at the entrance. No one sat next to me. They didn't want to disturb me. During the day Nayumich came to me, gave me some medicine, and promised to send me to the village with the field kitchen. The whole dugout smelled like tobacco. The faces of the soldiers looked gray because of the smoke. All I heard were cricket noises in my head.

"So, Klimich, you say we're going to get something out of this war. We don't need it, I tell you. Whether the Germans win or we win, we're going to have to work hard till our deaths. The problem is that we can't get land, and if we don't get it ourselves, then we'll never get it. The people are poor and needy and wild now, remember my words, there will be a big strike in Russia," Sasha warned.

Sasha finished speaking and leaned over to Klimich to light his cigarette. Chereshenko got involved in the conversation saying, "David Markovitch told us that we have to overthrow the czar so that we can govern ourselves, but we then asked ourselves: how can government run without a master?"

Zaporozhets, twisting his mustache, interrupted Chereshenko, "Don't you get it, stupid, that all the leaders will be picked from the working class, not from those who studied how to be leaders. You heard him, but incorrectly."

Chereshenko replied, "I got everything all right, Zaporozhets, I just can't say it like he did, he's got a head on his shoulders, and he sings as well as a bird! I just wish life could be that sweet."

"When you think about it, why are we fighting with the Austrians and the Germans? They're just obeying their own government. Well, the German, he really is angry, but the Austrians, they're going against us unwillingly," said Zaporozhets. He wiped his mouth with his arm and, looking around, waited for a response to his words.

Sasha started talking again, "I'll tell you this story, when I was sixteen I went to the village where my sister was married and now lives. It was the days of the Holy Trinity.[2] That is where I found out how bad the upper class can be. A landlord lived about five versts from this village. His face was round like the moon, and his stomach big as a barrel. A forest stretched for about twenty versts behind his mansion. I came to visit my sister and met this cute girl, Glashka. There was a celebration, and we went to it. We spent some time there and then ran off into the forest. We were young and just wanted to get away from the others. We walked and walked, and only God knows where we got to, kissing the whole time. The sun had already set. It smelled so sweet in the woods, and we walked as if we were drunk, then we lay down. The tree above us was big and beautiful. We lay there embracing, and then we saw a really old man. Glashka turned to me and said, 'Sasha, where is he going, he is about a hundred years old, he keeps a bee farm, but it is about three versts from here. Call him, Sasha. Maybe he is lost; his sight is really bad too.'

"We got up and walked to the old man, I asked him, 'Grandpa, where are you going?' He was silent. I thought he was deaf, so I said it again right above his ear, 'Grandpa, where are you going?'

"'To the landlord, to the landlord Nikolai Vitalievich,' he said.

"'His servant came and told me to go see the landlord because he wants to know why I gave him bad honey.'

"The old man sat down on a tree stump.

"'Is it much farther?' he asked us."

"What did you say to him, did you carry him on your back or something?" asked Chereshenko.

"No, I didn't carry him on my back, but we took him by the arms and led him toward the landlord's house. It wasn't easy, but we got him there," Sasha explained.

"Did you sleep sweet?" laughed Klimich.

"I'm not going to lie, it wasn't bad; I mean I did meet Glashka. I said good-bye to her and went with the old man to his landlord. My heart aches at this memory; I'll never forget it in my life. I wasn't too old back then, and this had such an impact on my mind. This guy walked out with a plate of honey, and it was blacker then black. The landlord came up to the old man, put some honey on his hand, and smacked the old man in the face with it. The old man fell on his knees. On the ground, he pleaded for forgiveness. 'Take him, Ivanich, take his old bones.' The guy led the old man to the shed; all the while the old man was silent. I hid behind it, but through a hole I could see everything. They pulled his pants down and were beating him with birch rods. My heart aches at the thought. His beard, his face, and his hair were all covered in honey, and the hay was sticking to him. The old man whimpered and babbled, 'My bees, my sweet bees.' And that was the last thing he said. And then he died."

Sasha shut up, and Nayumich walked in, looked at me and said, "Come on, you the sick one, I came for you."

I walked out with Nayumich through the trench, and we went to the village with the field kitchen wagons.

)))

The days passed by. I saw a lot of misfortune and very little happiness. In the barn, after emptying my pockets full of pears, I went to sleep on the hay. I thought about my conversation with David Markovitch. He of course told me the truth. I saw a lot of horrible things here and not much of anything good. But I tried not to think about that. I tried to avoid thoughts of life even though I understood now there are a lot of hardships in it. Every time I would think about someone else's problems, I wanted to cry. I just wanted to live a little longer without seeing the bad in everything and everyone. I tried not to think about the suffering of the dying soldiers. I remember, after a battle, in the dugout there was an injured Austrian, he was really young. I looked at him for a while, and then I imagined his mother. He probably had a mother who thought about him and waited for him to come home. I started to cry, and turning away from him, I tried to shrug off the heaviness of the scene. I left and went to my own dugout, where soldiers were playing the harmonica, and it was so merry. One of the scouts made a clown mask and danced on it. I started dancing with him, forgetting the dying soldier. In the evening when everybody left, I had a vision of the Austrian again, and I tried to get his face out of my head. I wanted to have fun with the others and laugh and not think about this. When I woke up, I remembered him again. I got up and started to get dressed. I bent down to get my boots, and there was that stupid mask. I grabbed it and threw it out.

)))

"Sit down, Sasha, here on this tree stump, while we wait for Zina. Why are you so glum?" asked Trofim.

"Is this called life, Trofim? You don't see a female for months. You start to miss them. A female is a soft," Sasha answered.

"You, Sasha, are the right kind of guy, don't complain. The only danger here is getting killed, other than that, you can do anything you want. I can't wait for Zina, but I have to ask her a favor, I need her to write a letter to Lipki, after all, she does write neater then you."

I walked out yawning.

"You were sleeping? We knocked on that little house, it didn't seem like you were in there. Your eyes are going to be swollen if you sleep so late. You're not worried about anything; everything is the same to you. You always walk around smiling. Come on, Zina, let's go into the hut, you can write my wife a letter. Come on, you're so lazy!" commanded Trofim.

Trofim hit me slightly in the back of the head as Sasha began to sing:

"Eh, what is this war for?
They fight in the mansions
They eat so much
But the people shed their tears!"

Without moving the blanket, Sasha sat down on my bed with his dirty boots. Trofim sat down in the corner on a bench under an icon decorated with paper flowers. The roaches moved onto the stove to keep warm. With his head bent over the table, Trofim picked out the dirt from the cracks in the table with the sharp point of a pencil.

"Well, think, Trofim, and I will write," I said.

At first I wrote all the customary greetings as I did for all the soldiers, occasionally asking Trofim the names of family members I didn't remember.

"You said all the greetings, now write about the serious stuff," he said.

My one and only, Klavdia Kasianovna, my heart aches because I miss you so much and I am so upset at your letter about the crops, since they aren't growing much. Something in my heart has been torn. My head feels heavy like iron. I have no appetite anymore. It must be terrible for you with Mashka and Vacya. My lovely Klavdia Kasianovna, I will tell you about a terrible dream I had last night. I slept on a cot in my hut, and a giant spider climbed all the way to my nose, spun out a bloody web, and wrapped my whole body in the red webbing. My whole body felt squeezed. I was so scared, I woke up and started to cross my chest and pray to God. This dream is definitely not a good sign, Klavdia.

Trofim stopped talking and sank into his thoughts after dictating these words. I drew circles on the page after putting the last period at the end of the sentence. Sasha snored loudly on my bed, and somewhere behind the stove a cricket chirped. Outside, the trumpeter Lykyanchenko sounded the call for duty on his gray horse.

CHAPTER 6

Zina's battalion marches to a new village through a terrible thunder
and lightning storm. There she visits an old mansion used as a
former Austrian headquarters.

Making a lot of dust, the advanced guard left. The regiment waited
until they got farther away. The battalions took a break at the end of the
village. The companies separated. No one put their rifles away, everyone held onto them. The enormous hot sun ever so slowly descended
to the horizon. It felt like its rays got under your skin. They melted
your insides.

Trofim sat in the shade by the fence taking off his boots. His black
hair was shining in the light, like a crow's jet black wing. Sasha was
trying to poke a ripe apple with the tip of his bayonet. The trees in the
private yard were filled with apples.

After drying his feet and his cloth foot wraps, Trofim put his boots
back on. "I could go for some water," he said with his lips parched, as
he started looking around. Along with his moving pupils, you could
see the little red webs of veins in his swollen eyes.

The country gentleman's house stood on the edge of the village.
Sasha walked lazily towards it with a group of soldiers following him.
They all wanted to drink. They stood by the gate for a long time, not
confident enough to walk in. Sasha separated from the group and
walked into the yard. In a minute, a worker came out with a bucket of
water. He didn't let the bucket out of his hands, but brought it to the

lips of each parched soldier. One by one, the soldiers drank from the hands of the worker.

"Stand tall!" yelled Sergeant "Crater," and the soldiers, wiping their mouths with their sleeves, ran to line up.

)))

In the distance, the advance guard was in a cloud of dust. They stretched out on the road making even more dust as they marched. Behind them was a line of guards that looked like it was made from rubber; it would stretch out and then get close together again.

The sun was heating us with its last surge of energy. It seemed as if it were melting in the air. The air was getting hotter and heavier. It became unbelievably hard to breathe. The companies moved drowsily.

"Singers, forward!" I heard the battalion commander order.

Trofim didn't sing, but he liked to listen to war songs.

"It lights you up inside," he would say. Right now he wasn't happy. When the singers started on "mountaintops, I see you again," he turned to his neighbor and said, "Only the devil would make people sing in this kind of heat."

"Be quiet, Trofim, as if you don't love hearing it," Sasha said laughing.

They sang, "Mountaintops, I see you again . . ."

Straining their voices, they sang. The rest of them joined in: "The Karpatski valleys, the grave of dashing fellows . . ."

The song was cut off on their chapped lips. In half an hour we had a short break.

"All right, let's go!" Captain Krapivansky ordered, with the much-too-familiar phrase. The soldiers blew their noses with one finger on a side of their nose. Everyone went into different bushes all along the road to do their business.

The marches didn't exhaust me anymore. I got more and more used to the marching life and was happy with my endurance. Soldiers now looked at me as an equal companion.

"It's not bad, you cleaned the rifle nicely. You have to wipe the bolt a little," commented Ivanov. He put my rifle back into place and looked at me with kind eyes, which before seemed so gloomy to me. He always looked like he was frowning at everyone.

We moved forward in half an hour. It was either the compliment from Ivanov or the little break, but I started cheerfully marching forward. Along the right side of the road little bushes appeared, and the farther we went, the more greenness there was. Soon it turned into a forest. There was a long winding road in the shade of the maple trees. In front of us a huge cloud arose as if something was blowing it up from behind the trees.

Not even ten minutes passed before the whole sky was completely filled with clouds. It got really dark. In the silent darkness, it seemed as if the trees were pressed against each other, frightened. It was like the wind was walking in soft slippers along the tops of the trees. Like a steam room, it got really hot in formation, and the soldiers, without permission, started unbuttoning their shirts.

"It's going to thunder," Trofim quietly uttered. As soon as he said the word thunder, a cold sweat washed over me. I stopped noticing the intolerable heat. Instantly I pictured my house. There when it began to thunder, I could close all of the windows and doors, and my bed was my savior. There was no bed here and certainly no windows or doors. There weren't any pillows to hide under. I was just about petrified. I pressed close to Trofim and took Sasha by the sleeve.

A fire lit up the forest and immediately died down. The forest looked white with radiance. The fireworks barely died down when somewhere nearby it sounded like a skyscraper collapsed. There were endless rumbles, and the thunder overtook everything and then with a crack disappeared into the depths of the earth. For a moment, it seemed that the regiment was floating in the air. After the first crash, somewhere in the distance, it sounded like single bricks fell with a deafening sound.

Trofim crossed his chest as he said, "Oh God, have pity on us sinners!" His face looked darkened.

I involuntarily yelled "Oh" and leaped over to the unenthusiastic Sasha. It seemed as if everyone's faces changed; their eyes got bigger, their noses looked longer, and they were serious. There was lightning and thunder in the distance. It kept getting nearer. We were awaiting a lightning strike.

It was as if an invisible sword cut through the clouds. The road became light like a spark of magnesium. For a moment we were all blinded. I closed my eyes. I was scared to open them. The loud thunder came from inside the forest. It got so light out. The battalion moved away from the forest. The formations were breaking up. The companies were frightened, and they were all mixed up. We were all moving forward in such disorder, something pulled me forward, and I wanted to hide somewhere. I would have rather seen a storm of bullets than hear one more rumble of thunder.

I ended up at the head of the battalion. Lieutenant Colonel Krivdin was pale as the moon. I couldn't believe that he was still walking. He told his orderly to walk at the head of the battalion with his horse. He turned around and was irked by the disorder he saw, shouting, "Devils!" The next thunderbolt hit, and it was so loud that nobody heard him.

Above Yerohin's bayonet was a lightning bolt that reached the sky. The whole first company gasped together. Krivdin stuttered. With a shaking hand, he crossed his chest and took out a picture of a saint from his pocket. He started kissing it with his blue lips. Black as coal, Yerohin lay on the ground. His black hand was clutching his rifle. His bayonet was now curved. On his unbuttoned chest lay a cross. "We should dig him a grave," said the soldiers.

The First Company sergeant walked up to Krivdin with a bashful step. "Sir, I request permission to put away our bayonets and allow the rifles to be placed on the ground."[1]

Krivdin regained his composure and responded, "What are these idiocies? You should know yourself what to do."

Behind the forest there was what sounded like a loud explosion. Two or three raindrops fell from the sky. Right after them, it began to pour. We breathed easier. The sky cleared up. Water poured through every little space in the sky.

Like a little chick, I ended up near Trofim again. He pulled his head into his shoulders, and his lips were continuously whispering something. It was as if he wasn't even there. I wanted to talk to him, but it was obvious that he wouldn't hear me. The soldiers continued to walk in disorder. I moved towards Sasha.

"Sasha, what's going to happen?" I asked him in a raspy voice.

"Everything already happened," he answered me. "It can't get any worse. Ilya the Prophet rode passed on his horse. The bitch hit our formation. Did you see the zigzags the lightning made? Ilya increases the force, and our Yerohin is dead from it."

Krivdin's horse, now at the head of the battalion, carried his limp, dry body. He had wrapped himself in a rubber poncho. Stepping through the sticky mess, his horse covered the first few rows of soldiers in dirt.

The soldiers were completely drenched. I felt like I was in a bucket of water. The drops got under my collar and trickled down my shivering body. The material soaked through and stuck to my body and my legs. The water trickled along my legs into my boots like cold caterpillars. Soon there was a sticky substance collecting in them like vaseline. I wanted to say something, but I couldn't. It felt as if not only my bones were soaked through, but my tongue too, and it was hard to move it. It was not only hard to speak, but also hard to walk. My boots sank into the ground. My feet were slipping, and it left long lines in the mud. After about another half hour, clumps of dirt were stuck to my boots.

There were voices heard in the ranks, "It would be nice if we could unroll our coats." Other voices caught on, "coats, coats," was heard throughout the whole battalion.

The officers were silent, as if they were dead. Captain Krapivansky moved to Lieutenant Colonel Krivdin and said, "They should unroll their coats. They are soaked."

"I won't allow it," said Krivdin, cutting him off. "They will have nothing to cover themselves with at night," he cautioned.

Accompanied by the persistent rain, the rows of soldiers trudged on. It got dark. The soldiers spoke and here and there lit cigarettes. The officers acted blind and deaf.

Trofim walked silently in thought. Maybe he was sleepwalking. His head was bopping around as if it were tied to his shoulders. All of a sudden, he slipped a little and then straightened up right away. The soldier in front of him started screaming. Those around him yelled, "Stretchers, stretchers!" The hurt soldier had a bayonet wound in his hip. It was from Trofim's rifle and bayonet. The sergeant ran up to Trofim and said, "You idiot, where is your brain?" And with those words, he raised his hand to hit Trofim. In the distance a sound was heard as if two trains had collided. The sergeant put his hand down and started crossing his chest. "Once an idiot, always an idiot," he said, and with that all his anger was gone. The soldiers were told to hold their rifles upright and bayonets rose up above the whole battalion.

In the darkness you could see the outline of the nearest village. Hundreds of dogs were barking there. Their barks greeted the advance guard. My chest breathed easier, my legs walked faster, and the air smelled of delicious soup.

The troop formations got thicker. Neighbors were glued to each other. Leg was by leg. Two legs walked as one. In the sticky dirt, there was the sound of a four-step march. Parts of the regiment walked into the village. The officers straightened up. Lieutenant Colonel Krivdin was yelling. All of a sudden someone in the Third Company started singing, "Rolls, rolls, rolls!" in a small voice.

The regimental kitchens were stationed in the church square. The cooks were busy all around them. People peeled mounds of potatoes over washtubs. There was smoke reaching up into the sky like a corkscrew.

The soldiers waited for their dinner in the square beneath the oaks. An accordion played "Barinya." Someone banged on a container with a spoon. Replacing each other, soldiers from the advance guard danced around.

)))

Three Stavropolian battalions replaced the Seventy-Fifth Stavropolsky Regiment, which went to rest. The Fourth Battalion of our regiment was held in reserve. The Fifth Company, which I was sent to, surrounded the mansion of Lord Bogusha in the shape of a horseshoe. Honeycombed with bullets, the white house with circular columns was carefully guarded by the lord's old servant.

I decided to look into the lord's house I had heard so much about. The sun was setting, but it wasn't dark yet. I walked through the never-ending rooms of the mansion. In one room you could tell it was used as the Austrian headquarters before the Russians arrived. There was a table in the middle of the big hall with torn papers, pencil shavings, and pieces of wax. The green tablecloth was saturated with dust, covered in stearin, and there was spilled ink too. On both sides of the table there were thin, tall chairs, which were all a mess. The columns in the hall were decorated with garlands of dried-up flowers. A piano stood by the oval window near the entrance to the blue room. The top of the piano was open, and you could see the piano strings. There was a picture of a woman in an old-fashioned, black bearskin army hat on the cover of the fallen music notes that lay on the floor. I opened the music notes and barely understood what it said:

From the prettiest Warsaw girls
We will form an Uhlan regiment.
One-Two-Three ... One ... Two ... Three ...[2]

I waved my hands and sang as I walked on. I sang pretty well, "One-Two-Three ..."

The wallpaper in the room of the lord's granddaughter was upholstered in thin, gentle pink silk. Broken glass cracked under my feet. An overturned perfume bottle was on the table in the powder room, which was covered in a blue veil. The pink bows on the side of the table were covered in powder. The powder and the puff were thrown on the floor. The silk curtains were falling off the window frames. In the corner there was a fireplace filled with piles of burnt letters.

The bed curtain was slightly opened, and there was a doll in a pink dress with a headscarf and a pink velvet jacket. There was a miniature rosebud in her black hair. The doll had proud, puffed-up lips and black eyes. I am going to take you with me. I am going to take you to the trenches, I thought. And still undecided whether I should take her or not, I went by the new motto I just learned, "One, two, three ..." and I grabbed the doll and ran out of the powder room. Now I had to get out of the mansion. I figured that I would see the rest later.

Hurry! I have to get out. It's getting dark out. I walked through the parlor and ended up in a long corridor. Now to the right, no, not here, this way. I pushed the door, this time into a small corridor. Now turn left, right. There were wooden crates filled with bottles blocking my path to the porch. No, I didn't come through here. I have to turn back. Where is the exit? It's getting dark, and I thought I'm not going to be able to find anything in these long corridors. The door to the park was right here, did I miss it? I was so confused. I was walking around in half darkness. Not important! There is nothing to be afraid of. But the mansion was quiet and creepy. Walking a little longer, I felt tired, as if I walked a couple of versts. Where did this winding staircase come from? It's probably the entrance to the mezzanine. I decided to sit down, relax, and try to remember the way I came in. I could have crawled out of the window of the pink room, why did I go here? I felt around in the dark.

A door creaked somewhere. I heard footsteps on the stairs. I hugged the doll. Creaking, a little door opened. The burning candles of a candelabra lit up an old man in a black frock coat.

"Mother Mary, Jesus Christ, the little Miss Zocya's doll is in someone's hands," cried the old servant. The old man's hands began to shake, and candles fell out of their holders. His slippers began to head in my direction. There was the loud sound of porcelain hitting the floor; the doll was broken.

Like a madwoman, I ran as fast as I could to the moonlit entrance of the hall. The old man's feet followed. I caught my breath in the hall by the window. The old man stood like a monument in the huge parlor room. His sideburns looked silver in the moonlight.

Jumping out of the window, I was on the porch. I was so happy. Yes, I was as happy as hearing the sound of an exploding bomb. In a few minutes I would see people. I will be among live people. I will hear their voices. Hurry! I put my hands on the white marble, pulled myself up, and jumped over the railing into the park.

)))

Soldiers secretly whispered about an underground passage under the lord's house that supposedly led to the Austrians. A few officers and several scouts searched the mansion. While searching through the attic, instead of finding arms, they found liquor bottles. They drank them and crawled through a window to the roof, where they got drunk. The mansion was under careful surveillance by the Austrians. The revelry of our officers didn't escape their watchful eyes. A shell sent their way quickly sobered them up and sent them rolling off the roof.

Returning to the trenches, the officers told Krivdin the story, interrupting each other, about how they risked their lives, found signal cartridges hidden by the servant they were sure he used to signal to the Austrians. Krivdin hit his knee with the palm of his hand and shouted, "Sons of bitches, bullshit sons of bitches!"

CHAPTER 7

Zina fends off the attentions of an amorous officer, Lieutenant
Zambor. She gets transferred to be a cavalry scout and on a mission
delivering a message, captures an Austrian soldier. Despite her
fears, she is accepted more as an equal with the other male soldiers.

There was roaring and unbearable clatter all around. Finally shells
replaced shrapnel, and their buzzing was a breath of fresh air for everyone. By evening, with a final groan, the cannons were silent.

"Here, take this to the regimental headquarters. The envelope
isn't sealed, bring it back, it's important," Lieutenant Colonel Krivdin ordered.

I always fulfilled my orders exactly, and I liked it that they would
send me with messages just like all the messenger men. Only Captain
Krapivansky sent me on these kinds of orders, but all of a sudden,
I had to carry a message from Krivdin. I didn't like the fact that he
smirked at me.

I had to get out of the communications trench and pass by the lord's
dark park to get to the headquarters in the lord's mansion. Countless
times I remembered that boy in Brody who said to me, "You are a girl,
they will not let you go to war," but now I am marching like a soldier,
I am carrying messages, and I know how to shoot.

It was a dark and starless night. You couldn't see anything five steps
ahead of you. Occasionally there was a gunshot. Silence. I walked
through a pine tree alley. The trees shuffled their black branches. The

park was gloomy and severe. Then an alley of linden trees began. They recently had bloomed, and the night still smelled of their spicy aroma.

I was curious as to what Krivdin wrote in the message. It was probably something important since he said it was urgent. What if I read it? Usually all of the envelopes were sealed, except for this one. I should read it and tell my friends the news. I got on my knees next to a tree and, lighting a match, I read: "The siren is buzzing. The dogs are howling. The servant is a spy. The Fifth Company is getting ready to attack."

What help? The servant is a spy? The dogs are howling? There is going to be an attack? I'm so confused. I lit a match again and read the note once more. That's what it says. I had to hurry to deliver the message anyway.

Colonel Zelinski came from the rear to replace Plakhov. He heard the jokes about his fear of fighting on the front lines. Zelinski read the message and laughed, commenting, "Read this. George Fedorivitch, Krivdin is seeing things; he needs a vacation to relax."

He gave the message to George, whom everyone loved. I soon left with the envelope to return back to my battalion.

)))

"Who's there?" I asked. I heard someone's footsteps. They were hurriedly moving toward me.

"I waited so long for you, Zinochka. Zina, listen to me," said Lieutenant Zambor. The night seemed even darker to me.

"I'm begging you, Zinochka, just kiss me!" he said. The lieutenant grabbed me and pulled me close to him.

"Leave me, how dare you!" I insisted, as Zambor knocked the rifle out of my hand unexpectedly.

"I will do anything for you, Zina. If you want, I will give you my horse Marquise," he said.

Marquise was a beautiful horse of English blood. No one in the whole division had such a horse as Zambor. Could that beauty really be mine? I wished to have any kind of horse, and all of a sudden Marquise could be mine! But in order to get Marquise, he is asking for a kiss. I imagined myself galloping on that beautiful horse, as Marquise easily and quickly gains distance. I imagined myself in a horse race and my horse comes in first place . . . applause . . . the orchestra plays music.

Zambor grabbed my head and started kissing my face. My fantasy quickly ended, and I was trying to get out of his grasp. I felt his breath on my face as he said, "You won't get away from me, you won't!"

I pushed Zambor in the chest abruptly.

"I won't let you go, I won't let you go. You hear me?" he repeated. He pushed my head back and covered my mouth with his palm. I heard someone cough nearby.

"Come here, Peter. Hold her. You'll get yours, according to our agreement," he said.

"Sir, Sir," replied a familiar voice close by.

I would have recognized the gloomy voice of Ivanov among a hundred soldiers. The same Ivanov whom I had such respect for and whose compliments made me so cheerful and energetic; artilleryman Ivanov whom I spoke to as my elder and expressed deep reverence toward.

"Come on, come on, drag her over here. I am telling you, you will get yours too," urged Zambor.

"Ivanov, how dare you! You and him both?" I yelled. It was the first time I was disrespectful to him.

"Help me!" I yelled louder. I smelled alcohol and the spicy aroma of the lieutenant, just like the linden trees in the alley. Zambor whispered something I didn't understand. All of a sudden someone breathed on me, and it smelled like tobacco and someone's strong arm yanked the lieutenant.

"You're not getting such a treat, you lout!" shouted Ivanov.

"Scoundrel, you lied to me; I will arrest you. You don't want to go through with it? And you interrupted me. Rascal. You are under arrest!" shouted Zambor.

"I went with you to defend her. You chose the wrong man, sir. Give me your hand, Zina. Let's go," said Ivanov.

He led me, holding my hand. I walked with him through the dark park. Blood rushed to my face, but he didn't see my blush of embarrassment, thankfulness and fault. Ivanov couldn't have done anything to make me disrespect him, but I suspected him of such a vile act as the lieutenant wanted to commit.

The envelope had two crosses marked on it. I brought it back, but Lieutenant Colonel Krivdin wasn't there. I gave it to Captain Krapivansky. He was on a bunk bed covered in hay, staring at the candle in front of him. His fur hat was all the way on the back of his head. His coat was covered in dry dirt all the way up to his waist. He turned his weathered face in my direction. His sharp eyes quickly ran over the envelope, and he said, "You can go now."

)))

Sunrise. There was no one in our living quarters. I was alone. I've seen myself in this cracked mirror hundreds of times, but it seems as if only now do I see the dark circles under my eyes, my eyes that look different. They used to be alive and laughing eyes, and now they looked dim. Disgusting eyes! You should have yelled and nothing would have happened to you! I scolded myself. No, you probably did the right thing, you shouldn't have yelled there.

I felt nauseous. But this will pass, I told myself, and picking up the mirror again I looked into it; again I saw my eyes, they were different, they didn't look like mine, as if they belonged to someone else. Don't look this way, I told them, I want you to look like you did before. Ugh! Everything is so repulsing. I threw the mirror and walked out of the dugout.

I walked through the trenches and felt like everyone was staring at me. I felt like they all knew last night's damn events. I tried to cover my face with my hand. I wanted to hide from all of the soldiers. My warm, slightly sweaty palm touched my cheek. I felt cold and dizzy. I sat down on the ground for a long time next to some soldier.

)))

Many days passed. Zambor didn't arrest Ivanov. The officers looked at me and laughed. Zambor walked among the officers satisfied and upon my approach he would whistle. The officers laughed loudly. Only Ivanov and I knew about the lieutenant's failed plan.

Twelve infantry scouts were transferred to become cavalry scouts. Sasha and I were both transferred. We were stationed five versts from the mansion. I was given a chestnut horse named Gnom, who had a white stripe on his forehead and a thick mane done in four braids. Sasha's horse, Cheremukha, stood next to mine in the stables. He was black, but his legs were white from the knees down. Zaporozhets got a horse, Panteleiko, who was chewing hay close by. After Chereshenko was done washing his horse, Belka, he came over to Zaporozhets and said, "Stupid, hey, Zaporozhets, change Panteleiko's hay. He's going to get black gnats."

Chereshenko scratched the back of his head and laughed, replying, "Well, what am I to do with such a small horse, even the chickens are laughing. When I sit on it, my feet drag along the ground."

We heard Sasha's enthusiastic laugh as he walked into the stable. He came up to Belka and petted him on the back, remarking, "It's not realistic to find a horse for you, Chereshenko. No matter what horse they give you, it will be too small. All you have left to do is ride camels. Let's go see the housekeeper, guys, she has bacon."

Everyone left. I was alone with Gnom. My horse moved his velvety head toward me and neighed. Panteleiko answered. I treated him to some sugar. I didn't know how to express my happiness to him. I wanted a horse for so long. I unbraided his hair and ruffled it up. I hugged his big face. Gnom breathed on me from his nostrils and drooled on my neck. I walked all around him, checking him from all sides. I wanted to braid his tail, but instead got a rough slap in the face. There was a sharp pain in my eye. I walked out of the stables, lay down on the hay and curling into a ball, went to sleep.

)))

The command, "To your horses," from Lieutenant Nikolsky, the cavalry scout leader, made everyone quickly jump and run to their horses. The soldiers called the merry Nikolsky, Akylka, due to his round figure, flushed cheeks, and upturned nose. Student Nikolsky, recently graduated from the warrant officers school, was wounded and then promoted to lieutenant.

"Forward march" and the scouts were off.

"Fly, my loyal friend," Nikolsky's tenor voice began and was cut off right away, as if he remembered all of a sudden he was at war.

We will be ahead of our advance guard. This isn't crawling on your stomachs, we are riding horses, and it's quicker. It would be nice to see Trofim. I miss him a little. You get used to a habit. Trofim is a good man, I thought.

We went three versts, and then Akylka led the scouts on a turn to Bogusha Park. Soon we met Zambor on his beautiful Marquise, with three other officers. They sang loudly, and you could tell by their voices that they were drunk.

Ringing our stirrups, we rode into the grove behind Bogusha Park.

"Rein left," commanded Nikolsky. The horses jerked to the side.

Under the old oak tree swung the dark body of a person; the head was drooping, and in the moonlight and the shadows of the leaves, looked like circling moths. I recognized the old servant. The wind blew his gray hair.

The reins fell out of my hands. I pressed my face into my horse's mane. With a jolt, my horse jumped forward.

"A spy hangs, let him hang," someone said.

"What did a person die for?" Sasha asked.

Zambor's drunken song was heard far away beyond the park and the grove.

The dawn covered the village like a blush. It was quiet and empty, only in the distance, on the road, a chicken bathed in dust, and somewhere the handle of a well creaked.

"If anything happens, hold on tight to the saddle and follow me, okay?" Nikolsky cautioned.

"There are a lot of us, what could happen?" someone asked.

"It doesn't matter that there are a lot of us. The Austrians have Hungarian horses, and they are quick," he replied.

A peasant woman ran out of her cottage into the street like a bird flapping its wings. Sasha ran up to her and asked, "Tell me what you want?"

"Have some sympathy, my daughter has been wounded, and the whole cottage is covered in blood. Oh God, help her, Moskaliki."[1] Sasha threw me his pack of bandages and said, "Here, Zina, wrap it around her and make it quick. If something goes wrong, I will whistle."

Inside on the floor, a little girl lay on straw. Blood poured out of her wounded arm, her face was pale, and her blue eyes dim.

"Mm . . . Mama," the daughter called. Her thin blonde braids were splashed with blood.

"Where did you come from, young one? You are only a child. How did you get with the Moskaliki?" asked the woman looking me over.

I bandaged the girl's arm tightly above the wound, as Nayumich taught me, and stopped the bleeding a little. A loud whistle from outside struck my ears. The only thing I could think of was that the Austrians had arrived and I was going to be captured. I ran out of the cottage as fast as I could, without finishing the bandaging of the girl's arm.

On the road, calmly standing there smoking, was the whole group of our scouts. At the sight of me they all burst into laughter, saying, "She got so scared! Ha-ha! She looks as pale as snow!"

I wasn't the least bit embarrassed, and I turned around and walked back into the cottage. When I finished with the girl, I asked for a pillow to put under her head. I was about to leave. The girl's eyes stared at me, and opening her little mouth, she laughed.

"Oh, my darling Ksana. Ksana, look at this young boy. Would you laugh at him? Do you feel better, my dear heart?" the woman asked her daughter. The girl turned her head and reached out to her mother. The mother's tears fell on Ksana's checkered apron.

)))

Battles have been going on for several days now. The most casualties were suffered by the Seventy-Third Krimsky and the Seventy-Fifth Kuban regiments. In our regiment, the Second Battalion suffered the most. The soldiers told stories of how, during the temporary command of Colonel Zelinski, during the height of battle, he attacked the Austrians, shouting, "Hooray." Zelinski was a little, self-assured, Polish man, well suited for the fight.

There were wagons on the road carrying wounded to the rear of the regiment. They were overloaded with the wounded. Some of them walked behind the wagons leaning on each other. I remembered the liquor in my canteen that Sasha had given me. I walked up to the wounded and asked if anyone wanted a drink. The soldiers reached for the canteen and soon enough emptied it.

"Zina," said a blond soldier, "David Markovitch, they killed him, tell the guys. Tell Gusev and give him this packet. It's some kind of papers. It's Markovitch's papers."

David Markovitch was dead. I didn't ask the soldier any more questions. Right next to me a scout was weeping and said, "I feel so bad, David was killed. They say he was torn to pieces by a grenade."

It wasn't that long ago I spoke with him. I saw his face clearly before my eyes. His death deeply affected me. I saw many dead and wounded people. It was often that you heard, "Egorov's hand was ripped off, Petrov's head was blown off by a shell, four soldiers were buried alive," and as terrible as it was, I was used to hearing these things. For some reason, when I heard about David Markovitch's death, I got really scared. I wanted to scream as loud as I could. The sudden fright passed, and all of a sudden I felt older. Something forced me to take action, and I consoled the soldier, saw Sasha, and shook his hand.

"Sasha, David Markovitch was killed," I said.

He stood there for some time staring at one spot, then walked away to the other scouts.

"Then he is killed. That's that," said Sasha, sighing deeply.

Chereshenko lit up a cigarette and said, "It's always like that in life, a good man gets killed during an act of bravery of some sort, but asses like Krivdin are getting fatter by the minute."

"He was a good man that David," said Zaporozhets.

I was left alone. The wagons creaked carrying the wounded to the rear of the regiment on the dark evening road.

)))

Klimich got a letter from his village of Nikitovka and before he even opened it, he gave it to me and said, "What do they write? Read it, Zina."[2]

"Sit, I'll read it to you," I answered.

To you, our dearest Vaciliy Klimich, I send my bows. It's been three months since I got out of the hospital. Now I walk around on crutches. They let me leave the army. They took a big part of our land away after we gathered the crops. The taxes are so high that we can't pay them. Before the holidays they took a spotted horse from Michael Kyrikov because he couldn't pay the taxes. His wife stood in the middle of the yard with one-year-old Aksutka and fell to the ground. She bowed to the tax collector on her knees. He showed no pity for the child in her arms and kicked Michael's wife in the breast. In the evening, the grocery store owner's servant took a bottle of vodka into town for the tax collector, and the priest's fat Praskovia put a roasted turkey on the table for him. They received special preference from him. Oh, brother, I don't understand why you are fighting this war. I cross my chest to the damp ground for you. The damned authorities torture us. Who needs this war for peasants' happiness? We can't take it anymore. To you, brother, I write with my greatest respect, your closest relative, Kuzma, Klim Gavrilovitch's son.

Klimich took the letter and hid the envelope in the lining of his service cap.

"Klimich, who brought you the letter?" I asked.

"My fellow countryman who came back to the trenches. Let's go, our scouts have gathered," he added.

The scouts were gathered near the church gate with Lieutenant Nikolsky. Seeing me, Akylka waved his arm and shouted, "Gusev, Zaporozhets, Zinaida, come here!" The three of us all received assignments. We were sent to the artillery battery and to regimental headquarters. I had to bring the lieutenant's report to the regimental headquarters. From what they gathered from a prisoner, the Austrians were in trenches two versts behind the village of Simki.

I hid the envelope in my jacket, closing it tighter. Nodding to the lieutenant, I kicked my horse and galloped away. I heard Akylka scream: "Go, go!" and realizing it was directed towards me, I made Gnom run faster out of the village.

Right behind the village there was a young forest. The golden autumn grove shuffled to the right of the road. The maple leaves bustled. The forest smelled like spicy soil and mushrooms. A flock of geese flew by very low. We went past this road at sunrise, and I remembered it well. Turning onto a narrow road to get to the farm faster, and thinking that by Akylka's reasoning I should be arriving, I slowed down. My horse bent his head toward his chest and getting hit in the face with a branch, he kicked his back legs up so high I barely held on.

The enemy was sending shrapnel shells through the forest to the road leading to the farm. The fire became more rapid. Being alone during the firing felt ten times scarier, as if they were all aimed at you. Being scared for yourself paralyzes you. You feel completely different when you are among others. Only here at war did I learn how strong a person's fortitude is. I remember distinctly how when we were in our positions by Kolpin someone said, "Thank God, the fire is directed towards the Twelfth Division now."[3] And then, "Thank God they stopped firing at us, now they're shooting away at the Kubans." And I remember when a soldier near Klimich was killed; the look on his face, besides fear, was one that said, "At least it didn't get me."

But everyone is in the same danger as their neighbor. It's as if people felt relief when the fire was directed away from them. Maybe later they felt ashamed. If they did, no one ever said anything.

A shrapnel shell exploded really close by. My horse seemed to shrink back and then all at once ran off wildly. Branches were hitting my face. It was really painful, and I didn't expect their force. Pulling on the reins, I got the horse to walk. The hiss of a shell was nearing. The explosion was a few feet away from me. Rattling, a fragment of it hit a tree, and then the young birch was in pieces. How can I get through the forest? How do I escape the artillery? I will probably die here. The battery was repeatedly firing. I have to move forward. Finally the fire was aimed to the left, and I pulled on Gnom's reins, and he walked through. All of a sudden Gnom looked around cautiously and pricked up his ears.

"Gnom, you pig, don't scare me like that, I'm already scared!" I yelled.

Going a little farther, I saw smoke behind the bushes.

"Gnom, stop moving your ears. A little more and we will get to our lines, and we will finally reach the farm and the headquarters."

Smoke was still coming from the bushes. Someone is probably smoking, I thought. Maybe I should go around the bush? Sasha would probably not be scared. No, enough being afraid. Taking out my revolver, I jumped over to the bush. The leaves of the acorn bush slowly parted, and an Austrian gradually appeared. My heart practically stopped.

"Guten Tag!" said the Austrian.[4]

I immediately remembered walking home late from my girlfriend's house, and turning the corner I met a drunken guy. Ignoring my fear, I bravely walked up to him and trying to be as polite as I could, I asked him, "Could you please tell me how to get to the seaport?" The drunk was very surprised and happy that someone took him for being sober, and he politely answered, "Madame, you go here and then turn left. Excuse me." Then speaking to the German in French, I hoped he would understand, "Camarade, voulez-vous etre prisonnier de guerre?"[5]

The young and smiling Austrian raised his hands and answered, "Ja, Ja!"

I put my revolver into the leather messenger bag and he handed me his clean carbine. He looked at me and handed me his canteen. I turned the cap and smelled rum. I then closed the cap, but tightly held the carbine.

"Je vous en suis reconaissant," I said to the prisoner and gave him back his canteen.[6]

My politeness seemed strange to the Austrian, and with a smile he asked if I was a cadet. I understood him, but I couldn't answer in German, so I started shaking my head laughing. He stared at me, and then his gaze fell on my hands. He jumped toward me, and taking my hands he yelled, "Mädchen, Mädchen!"[7] I thought this was so funny, I laughed out loud, and my laugh rang through the forest.

Letting the prisoner go in front of me, we moved on. I had to stop my horse often, because the Austrian kept turning around and looking at me. He walked slowly, tiredly dragging his heavy boots on his thin legs. I said to him, "You know what, get on the horse, and we will ride together. Sit." We rode together in silence, each one of us emerged in our own thoughts.

Arriving at the headquarters, I explained everything to the soldiers. Everyone laughed at me. They took the prisoner away. I felt bad parting with him. He looked like Sasha. He had the same blue eyes.

The division commander and his aide sat in a small yard. After catching sight of me, they both got up and walked towards me. Gnom, seeing the other horses lined up, started to get fidgety and pull on his reins. The officers neared the prisoner. I took the letter out of my coat and gave it to the aide. Looking at the envelope, he looked at the time and joked, "I see this was urgent. It was delivered late."

"I took this Austrian prisoner, and here is his gun. I got held up because of him. It's my fault." I explained.

"Which one of you captured whom? It's dark, and this letter that you brought was important, plus there was fire in the forest. Job well done, Zina, you can go rest," the aide replied.

They began questioning the prisoner. The usual questions, what division and how many and what kind of troops did they have in the reserve? He didn't speak, just silently stared at me. I turned around and went by my horse. I took out a roll that Ksana's mother gave me and bit into it. Right next to me, Gnom ate his hay.

)))

The regiment took up their positions. I showed the arriving reinforcements around. There were two new officers next to me. You could hear the ruffling of their new clothes. They just got out of the junior officers' school. At the sound of a bullet, one of them bent down and seeing a smile on my face, he blushed, and the next time a bullet fired, he bent down again, but this time he pulled his boot up. I looked at him, and there was an expression on his face that said, "You were wrong, I wasn't scared of a bullet, I was just fixing my boot." We walked on, and when a bullet struck near my feet I got scared, but I hid it well. I wanted to show all the guys that I was a woman and not afraid, and all of you men shrug at the sound of every bullet.

"She's showing us an example, guys. Isn't that right, Zina? Don't mind the fact that she's a girl. As soon as I get home, I'm going to teach my Katie to shoot. Mark my word. And David Markovitch, God bless him, he used to say the same about her. Let her get used to it, he would say. Let her learn to shoot, and we will see what happens," Bashmakin remarked, as he puffed on his cigarette.

CHAPTER 8

Zina and Sasha claim feelings for each other. Zina changes her outlook about the war. She no longer wants adventure but wants to stay in place. She likes the camaraderie with the other soldiers.

The stove in the cottage was smoking. The smoke was eating my eyes out. I went to the barn and got ready for bed. The evenings got chilly. The cold autumn wind tore at the straw roof. I covered myself with my coat. I wasn't alone for long. Sasha came into the barn and sat down next to me. We talked for a long time.

"I tell you, Zina, it's not easy for us. What do we make? They use our brothers, they use us, you understand? You think I don't make a lot? I am a fine mechanic," he pointed out.

Night came early in autumn. Whistling, the wind howled. Occasionally there was gunfire. Sasha moved to me and said:

"Zina, I've been meaning to tell you, I really like you. I am serious. Be gentle with me, Zina. I will remember your affection. I don't need anything from you. You know here at the front lines there are all kinds of people. You are the only one I like, and I am very interested in you. You aren't from our social class, and your manners are so soft and good. David Markovitch had been telling me for a while you will grow up to be a good person, that you are not a stranger to us even though you are not like us."

There was a heartfelt genuineness in Sasha's words. But as soon as he took my hand, I blushed, and I pulled it away.

"Zinochka, kiss me." His face came closer to mine, he smelled like berry soap.

"Zina, give me your kiss, don't be repulsed by me. I used the best soap just for you."

I touched his curls with my hand, and his hat fell off.

"You have a hand like silk, Zina, play with my curls."

I pet his curls, and I felt happy. The night was dark, there wasn't a star out. I kissed Sasha's blue eyes. I loved those eyes.

"Move closer, Zinochka, lie down and relax, don't tire yourself. Zinochka, you crept into my heart. I don't know what to do. You lit a fire inside of me."

I moved away from Sasha, his gentleness was clouding my head and making my heart pound. He sat near me and spoke of his family. He spoke a lot of St. Petersburg. I willingly listened to him. All of a sudden, I had this desire to grab him and hug him. I leaned toward him, puckering my lips, and my hand crept up his sleeve. My hand touched his warm body.

"Sasha," I said.

"Zina, what's with you? What are you doing? What do you want, Zina?"

"Nothing really," I replied.

"Well, if it's nothing, then don't touch me, it's not good to touch for no reason."

"You're the one that asked me to kiss you," I replied.

"Yeah, I did, but I want to explain everything to you. Open yourself up to me, open your heart and soul, and then if you want, we can get closer," he explained.

"Okay, Sasha, I'll tell you everything, where I grew up, who my parents are, everything."

I got up off his knees and sat down next to him and said: "Well listen, I'm starting. Once upon a time there lived a girl named Zina Kramsk..."

"Come on, without the jokes, tell the story."

"All right, listen, once upon a time..." I began again.

"Hey, who's there? Come out. Hurry up, Aria, get out, what are you doing in there? The horse, hurry up! Don't forget to release the saddle strap," Zambor shouted from outside. I got closer to Sasha. I hated the lieutenant. I was nauseated by the sight of him.

"Why are you shaking, Zina? Don't worry, I won't let you be harmed. Where the hell did he come from?" Sasha wondered.

The bright beam from a flashlight ran across the walls. Zambor shined the light on Sasha and me.

"Spending too much time with the volunteer," he remarked.

Zambor touched Sasha's shoulder with his stick. "You're too slow! Move faster!"

Sasha left, and I was walking out of the barn. Zambor blocked my path.

"We haven't seen each other in a while. Good evening, Zina."

"I'm not Zina to you, but a soldier. Let me walk past."

"Ha-ha-ha! But of course, soldier, just come here, don't struggle. I am drunk tonight, and I want you to be with me."

"Don't touch me, get away, I will complain!"

"Complain! Tell them. I'm not afraid of anyone. Get over here! You'll complain later."

He wrapped his arms around me. I punched him under the chin with all my might.

"Again hit me again!" he said, as he pushed my head back and kissed my face.

"Should I unsaddle Marquise or will you ride on, sir?" Sasha's voice suddenly announced.

Zambor let me go, whispering in my ear: "You're not going to get away from me tonight, I will find you!"

He turned around and walked out of the barn. I was left alone with Sasha. Zambor pulled up the saddle strap himself, got on the horse, and rode away.

"So, this is how it is, Zina, you have something going on with the officer. Well, what can I say? I'm sorry I interrupted. It wasn't me you were waiting for in the barn, it was the officer. Well, of course, he's cleaner than me and probably uses better soap, and it's someone like Zambor too."

"Sasha, what are you talking about? I hate him! Sasha stay with me, I will tell you everything."

"Don't lie to me. I'm not one who will listen. I thought you were different. You have relations with the officer. Stay here, wait for him; he will come to you. Get away from me! Just get off!" he yelled.

Sasha was so wrong, and Zambor was disgusting. Everything that happened made me so mad, and I cried. I ran out of the barn, ran to the stable, saddled up Gnom, and rode to the village of Koropets, where our Sixth Artillery Battery was located.[1]

)))

In the morning the battery commander, Bashkirov, invited me to come to the observation post with him. In the forest, after climbing the ladder up the tree to the post, Bashkirov asked me if I wanted to give the commands.

"You can command, Zinochka, would you like to? Look here," he said.

I looked into the periscope, at the end of the forest near the Austrian position, little figures moved around.

"All right, Zinochka, command!" he said. And stretching out the phone to me, he said: "Say it, hurry, ready . . . aim . . . fire!"

I repeated the commands. I heard the fire. I saw the shrapnel explode over the forest.

"It didn't make it! Too bad! We'll send a shell, fire again!" Bashkirov urged me on.

"Fire again!" said Bashkirov, and his words kept me going. I felt a burning desire to hit the target. Changing the distance, I gave the commands again. He bent over the periscope again.

"Perfect! We got 'em! Look! Stay with us, Zinochka. What's the infantry to you, do you really want to stay in the trenches?" he asked, trying to persuade me.

I looked into the periscope. The chaos that now arose in the Austrian trenches was obvious. They ran out of the forest, then back, in their little blue-gray uniforms.

The battery didn't fire anymore. We left the observation post, and saying farewell to the artillerymen, I distinctly heard Bashkirov say to another officer: "She liked shooting. We'll lure her over. You think she will come?"

I went back to my regiment with a doubled anger at myself and everyone surrounding me, with a terrible guilty feeling from my actions at the observation post, firing at the Austrians, and a completely lonely feeling. My Gnom rode quickly. I got a whiff of evaporated human blood with the freshness of the first frost. It was the smell of the front lines. Maybe that was when, for the first time, I realized the absurdity of this war. I couldn't forget the smile of the Austrian. A cold sweat came over me. My horse galloped. My ears rang from his running fast and the autumn wind.

)))

I was dragging the bucket of water for my horse as I met Sasha along the way. He walked past, not even noticing me. When everyone was resting, I tried to get to the scouts Sasha would be with. He didn't pay any attention to me, and that made me like him even more. During the march we were so close; I looked at his blue eyes, his slender figure, his broad shoulders. It was as if I stopped existing to him. If I asked him something, he would answer late or not answer at all. When he would leave with a message, I would wait for him. Even though he wasn't speaking to me, his presence was comforting, and when I'm with him, I'm not afraid of anything. Last night he came back, unsaddled his horse, and went to sleep. In the middle of the night he got up, fed his horse, came into the cottage where I slept, sat on the bench, and was writing something until sunrise. But he didn't utter a word in my direction, even though he knew I was awake. I came up to him and asked: "Why are you silent?"

He looked at me and said: "You are a stranger to me, you're involved with the officer, get away from me!" and he turned around.

I didn't know how to soften him up. One time I went to the stable and washed his horse. Then I sewed buttons on his shirt. He never noticed. Sometimes he would curse an extra few times in front of me. I couldn't stay mad at him for long. All I wanted was to hear a kind word from him and for him not to view me as the officer's means of enjoyment. Finally, Zambor went away on leave, and I got some peace.

I caught up to Sasha and decided to stop being afraid of him, giving my horse water at the well.

"Sasha, stop. Stop, I tell you!" I shouted.

He stopped, and his bright lips were twisted.

"What?" he replied.

I explained: "Listen, Sasha, you told me you wanted my soul, then why don't you do something about it? You don't even want to listen to me. Is that the way to be? Who are you making yourself out to be? Even if I was with Zambor, what do you care? If you love me already, then love me for real, as if you don't follow plenty of girls around. So you see . . ."

Chereshenko and Zaporozhets walked up to the well. Untying his horse, Sasha went off with them. I was left there standing alone. I felt a distancing from him. If he were to come back right now and offered a kind word, I would turn away from him. The feeling I once had for him would never be the same, even though I liked him a lot.

)))

I saw Colonel Plakhov up close for the first time. He had just returned from vacation. Strong and sturdy like an oak tree, he held a fat, wooden stick with a metal tip in his powerful hand. His left hand scratched his short hair. He wiped his pointy nose with a white handkerchief. With his little rat eyes darting, he searched for someone. Noticing his soldier servant, he smiled. He was happy to see him with a bottle of iodine. He went into a hut, leaning on his wooden stick.

"Oh boy, does he drink that iodine to strengthen his system," the servant explained to the other servants.

Sasha came back in the evening from the Fourth Artillery Battery, where he had gone to deliver a message.

Just as in the trenches, I was always amazed by the attention of the surrounding scouts. If I took off my shirt or my trousers, everyone would turn away or one of them would shield me with their uniform. I got used to this method of changing, just as the soldiers did. Before that, I used to change under a coat. My neighbors noticed this, and Trofim first offered, saying: "I will stand by the door, cover it with a uniform, and you can change. It's so irritating to sleep in all those clothes."

Three of us scouts were rooming together in a little hut. Here with us resided a young woman with three children. We slept on the floor. My body couldn't rest on such a hard surface. Soot from the tiny lantern would clog our nostrils. A baby started crying in its cradle. The mother got up, leaned over the child, yawned, and let it suck on her breast. The crying stopped. The woman stood there for a little while and then got into her bed again. Her wide foot slowly rocked the cradle over my head; finally it stopped. The baby slept. Her foot fell from the cradle and hit the bed heavily. The woman stretched and began to snore.

Next to me soldiers with their mouths open. Without any movement, next to me lay Sasha's head of curly hair. The hay under him was getting wet from drool. I heard a strange ruffling sound. I looked under the table, but there was nothing there. I put my head under the bed, and there was a huge black mass moving towards us. They were big cockroaches. I jumped up and sat down at Zaporozhets's feet. Along his neck, there was a little, black, moving chain.

"Zaporozhets, wake up, the roaches are coming!" I shook him, and he woke up and looked at me surprised.

"Are you crazy?" he answered.

"Roaches, Zaporozhets, they're eating you," I said.

"Why aren't you sleeping?" he asked.

"I'm scared," I replied.

"Go to sleep," he said.

Zaporozhets twisted his mustache, turned over onto his other side and began snoring. Black masses of those things engulfed the sleeping ones. I picked up my coat and went outside. I lay down at the door.

)))

The cavalrymen were on their way, illuminated by the sunrise. In one day the Stavropolsky Regiment left the Austrians a few versts back. The companies moved into the Austrian lines at the Sinavinsky Forest. We were moving along with the regimental headquarters. We were nearing the village of Guta Penyatska.[2] Behind us was a group of military policemen. The junior sergeant of the police group, Dybelo, tall and broad-shouldered, proudly thrust forward his chest, which was decorated with the medal "For Effort." Old Rashpil walked by his side. Their faces were so similar. They both had wide noses, and their faces were marked with smallpox scars. In their front rows, there were about six soldiers who stood out as well, because they had had the same sickness. The soldiers called the police group, "the Rashpil group."

))⟩

My horse started limping after the march, and after bringing him to the stables for the vet to see, I went back to the dugouts. The wood was crackling, and a bright flame lit up our living quarters. Klimich was helping me clean a herring.

"So, tell me, Zina, why aren't you going home? You go through all our hardships. Why do you do it? I wouldn't dream of it. Even though you've gotten used to a soldier's lifestyle, I can't understand why you insist on staying here."

This wasn't the first time the soldiers asked me such a question, and I didn't have a real answer for anyone. When I left home, I was led by a childish fantasy. I always had a thing for wild adventures. One time I planned to go to America with three of my friends. I guess it was the same at fifteen, when I had a desire to go to war. I desired change and adventure. Back home some of our neighbors were soldiers. I watched them for hours, amazed by what they were doing. I was especially intrigued by the horsemen of the Kargopolsky Dragoon Regiment. I knew a lot of soldiers there. I was at their stables quite often and treated the soldiers to tobacco I stole from my father. In exchange for the tobacco, they let me see the horses. My mother and father were horrified every time we sat down for dinner, and I smelled of horse manure. When the war started, I wanted to go with the regiment.

When I used to look at pictures of battles, my imagination ran wild. But apparently the pictures showed very little truth. There was one that stuck out in my memory. There was a Cossack drawn on it, with a sword, on his gray horse galloping toward the barbed wire. There were gray-haired generals who were on their way to attack, and priests who walked ahead of the lines holding up crosses. That was in the pictures, but life on the front lines drew different pictures for me.

I knew that every one of the soldiers would leave this place, would run away, but I stayed. I couldn't leave anymore. I was used to the people. It was hard to simply part with them. I met new people here and now understood a different way of life. Sometimes something urged me to go home, to tell them about everything.

One time at home, the doorman came to see our nanny in the kitchen. I heard him cry and tell her all about his grief:

"Alekseevna, think about it, they drove my last son away to war. How will I, an invalid, go on without them? Do people even come back from there? I keep aging. Maybe I won't even see them ever again."

I didn't understand why the old man was crying. His son was going to be a hero. It was a holiday. My father walked into the kitchen. He gave the doorman a coin. He stood by the doorway, but didn't leave.

"His son, Vacya, was drafted to fight in the war," Alekseevnushka explained.

"You should be proud. He will fight for his country, the motherland. That's great," said my father. My father turned around and walked out of the kitchen. The old doorman crumpled a cap in his hands. No one spoke to him anymore. He quietly opened the door. In the doorway by the carpet he dropped the holiday gift from my father, a silver ruble coin.

Maybe when Zambor beat up Klimich, he didn't think he was causing him any pain. Lieutenant Zambor knew only one thing: he beat up a soldier.

"Zina, you are practically like my Ulianka, just as dark, but the younger one, she's different, she's really pale. I don't know how she got into our family," Klimich remarked, looking at me attentively.

"Here, Zina, I took it out for you." Trofim took a little handkerchief out of his pocket and handed it to me.

"Why are you so deep in thought, Zina?" Sasha asked. He took my hand and gently ruffled my hair. Lately he was nicer and more attentive to me.

)))

Like before, I remained in the trenches. I was a scout, just like before. I carried the same little envelopes with one or two crosses on them. Not a lot of time had passed since I left home. My wish to fight on the front lines was now substituted with a wish to stay right where I was. Months in the war felt like years. I changed a lot, and that whole yearning to serve on the front lines was replaced with a different mood.

I was alone here, one among hundreds of men. I liked the upper hand I had over a lot of other women. During our marches, the nurses looked at me, and in the villages, women and children ran out to get a look at me. One time, I saddled a young gray horse that had not been ridden and rode him around the village. The horse paid attention to all the village horses, and when I crossed the bridge, I met a guy returning from the fields. The horse walked calmly at first and then swiftly turned back. I pulled on the reins as hard as I could, but couldn't tame the horse. It ran around in hectic circles. I yelled to the guy, "Speed up!" He cracked a whip, and his horse was off, but the untamed horse didn't calm down. He ran after the other horse. I pulled on the reins and kicked him hard in the sides. He didn't listen. In one moment the gray horse's front hooves were right behind the other one's. The horses ran on. The guy sat hunched over. A crowd was gathering. I pulled the reins to one side with force. The gray horse was infuriated, and walking backward, he suddenly turned around at one point. One more second and I would have been squashed by him. Instinctively, I bent my whole body forward. The gray horse, shaking its head, calmly stood in one place. An old man of about seventy, my landlord and a participant of the Turkish war, came out of the crowd.[3] The old man came up to me and said: "What a girl, what a girl, she's a fiery one!" I really liked that.

One time in one of our battles, when we moved forward, the enemy quickly forced us back, and we started to retreat. There was a wounded man on the field whom I ran to. The male nurses came to him with stretchers, but when the enemy neared, they left him there. I ran after them and grabbed one by the sleeve, yelling at him: "You should be embarrassed. You have to help the wounded man!" He ran to get the stretchers and later when the battle was over, he told the other soldiers about me and told them about his cowardly act.

Now after a while, I was getting tired of this kind of life, but I still didn't want to go home. I had a strong attachment to these soldiers, to the regiment. I also liked it that everyone was used to me, too. Everyone found some kind of comfort in my presence. I walked through the trenches, and the soldiers greeted me with smiles.

Trofim bought me two handkerchiefs, and Nikolsky sent me a jacket from the hospital in Odessa. Everyone that came back from leave brought me gifts. I liked my position here. I got used to this life, as well. The scouts, the nobility of the army, as the soldiers called them, respected me and felt especially comfortable around me ever since one night in the trenches when Zaporozhets was telling a story and cursing terribly. Chereshenko told him to go a little lighter on the cursing, and then I cursed everything out myself for the first time. They all laughed, and ever since then we have been close.

I brought happiness to the lives of all the people that sat here who didn't see anything, but this terrible gray life of the trenches. This made me so happy at times.

CHAPTER 9

There is a time lapse. Zina's unit moves to Rokitno, about 185 kilometers northwest of Guta Penyatska. She is sick with the Spanish flu. Her unit is next at the nearby Dolzhok Forest. Sasha proposes to her, and he leaves for St. Petersburg. Zina's unit marches 30 versts and occupies Austrian trenches.

The snow fell unexpectedly early. It fell in big shaggy flocks. I lay sick in the officers' quarters. The doctors called my sickness "Spanish flu." Heat burned my throat, my temples throbbed, and I felt like there were crickets inside me.

There wasn't much left of the village of Rokitno.[1] The soldiers from the wagon trains settled into the dilapidated huts and sheds. The doctors took me with them into the little schoolhouse. There was no teacher. He abandoned his nest a long time ago in search of new refuge. The village school was abandoned, and snow covered the porch. The strong wind scattered the thatched roof. A black rooster slept at the doorstep of his lonely home. There was no child's laughter heard in this village, and no one played in the snow.

Occasionally a peasant woman would be walking with buckets, and a puppy would run whimpering after her and then return to its doghouse. The gates opened. It was the school guard driving a cow to the water hole. The cow's skinny body was cold. It barely moved its legs.

I lay on a foldable bed. Ivan Ivanovitch Morozov, a regimental doctor, and Dr. DeMorrey took turns taking care of me. The doctors played

Preference all day long.[2] I didn't understand anything about their boring card game, and I got sick of being here. I wanted to go outside where it was cold.

The gloomy days dragged on. They played the same game from dawn to dusk and from dusk till dawn again. In between games they would take care of me, and it seemed to me that they did it out of boredom. I got better surrounded by their attention.

Putting on my coat and fur hat, I went out into the corridor in the evening. Here DeMorrey's servant was fanning the samovar with the top of his boot. He wiped his eyes with his free hand.

"Did you get dirt in your eyes, Nikolai?" I asked.

"No," he replied.

There were tears streaming down his face. Quietly sobbing, he told me the whole story. He got a letter from home. His brother-in-law told him that his son died, the only worker left in the family, and his wife, Anisa, took in an Austrian prisoner for help. She was tired of waiting for her husband on the long lonely nights, and the Austrian became her lover. Now everyone points and laughs at her growing belly.

The water boiled in the samovar. Nikolai pulled on his boot and carried the samovar to the doctors. I slowly walked out into the yard. The snow was crackling under my feet. Bare trees swayed in the wind. Pigeons were huddled up at the door of a stranger's home, where a nest had been abandoned long ago by starlings headed south. Nikolai stood leaning on the picket fence, with a jacket on his shoulders, holding his head in his hand as he stared at the starlings' nest. Myriads of snowy sparkles flickered.

Morning; they keep playing their card game. Morozov was quickly shuffling the cards. Young doctor Arhipov was scratching his dirty hair on the back of his head. DeMorrey was sharpening a pencil. The game was starting.

Wrapping cookies up in paper, I was ready to leave the doctors' house and return to the trenches. I spent a few hours in the veterinary section of the stables with my sick Gnom. I fed him sugar cubes, giving him everything I had. Gnom wasn't getting any better, and his leg was swollen.

Saying my farewells to the doctors and feeling the electric flashlight that Arhipov gave me in my pocket, I walked out the door. Hearing the sound of a propeller, I quickly returned to the doctors.

"It's a German airplane!" I blurted out.

"Maybe it's ours. Why do you think it's the enemy's?" Arhipov asked in a frightened tone.

We ran outside. The plane was flying really low over the village and circling around the church. It flew closer towards our street.

"They're going to start dropping bombs. Underground quick!" shouted a doctor.

DeMorrey went, and everybody followed him. A minute hadn't even passed when there were loud noises heard nearby. The ground started falling in the cellar. For a second we didn't understand anything. We sat there huddled close together and silent.

"Ivan Ivanovitch, if we are going to sit here for so long, it's a shame we didn't take the cards along," DeMorrey commented, ruining the silence. Arhipov and I laughed out loud.

"We don't have time for them now. What kind of fantasy is that, doctor?" asked Morozov, while lighting his little pipe.

We heard the mooing of a scared cow coming from the yard.

"'What happened? You should look, Ivan Ivanovitch," DeMorrey suggested, nudging Morozov.

"What do you think? I'm scared to take a look? Let's go, Zina," Morozov replied.

We pushed the little door. A burning smell came through to the cellar.

"We're on fire!" yelled Morozov, in a wild voice.

Everyone ran after us. The little schoolhouse was in flames. The fire moved from the neighboring shed. A bomb was dropped about forty paces from the cellar.

"What kind of shit is that? Dropping bombs on peaceful neighborhoods?" asked Ivan Ivanovitch, appalled.

The sound of the propeller was gone. The doctors ran to their house. The servants started running through the yard. The old man was pulling his cow by its horns. The rooster sat at the door of the henhouse as before, with one foot under its wing.

DeMorrey was the first one to get into the house. He threw their belongings out the window: boots, shoes, pots, pillows, blankets, books, and glass containers; everything was thrown away. The flames were getting bigger and bigger. A huge wooden log fell, erupting in flames. Windows were cracking. The flames licked the sides of the little house. All of a sudden Morozov ran into the flaming house.

"Ivan Ivanovitch, where are you going, what's with you?" yelled DeMorrey, after him. But the doctor was already inside the house. At this time, beams were falling one by one.

"He died!" said Arhipov, who sat down in the snow. He whispered: "He died, Ivan Ivanovitch died."

But Ivan Ivanovitch didn't die. He ran out of the burning house covered in soot. Opening his shaking hands, he showed us the cards with burnt edges.

)))

In the morning an order was given for all of the scouts to return to the trenches. The wagon drivers stayed with the horses.

"They've completely exhausted us; go here, go there. I heard they are going to transform our group," Klimich remarked.

Lieutenant Nikolsky went into the trenches with us. The snow was falling, covering the ground with a white layer. A lot of snow had fallen overnight. Bent-over soldiers were shifting from one foot to the other in the trenches.

"It's pretty harsh that they don't give us gloves," Klimich complained.

During the day the Austrians opened fire on the Twelfth Division. They said that the enemy wanted to fight for the Dolzhok Forest that was under our control, but our artillery wasn't silent either and was constantly firing at the Austrians.[3]

The sappers arrived at night. They told us about our listening posts and said that the Austrians were supposedly passing a mine gallery our way. Krivdin told Plakhov about the rumors of the oncoming underground attack. All the soldiers whispered, and everywhere one word was heard, "tunnel." We couldn't sleep; we listened. The long winter night seemed ten times longer. Everyone thought that any second everything would blow up. Everyone was charged and tense, and at night when quacking sounds were heard from mines near the Twelfth Division, everyone thought it had begun. But a little time passed, and the explosions would stop. The soldiers were exhausted and slept uneasily.

A bright sunny day was dawning on us, and the fear was disappearing. Life in the trenches resumed. Starting their work, soldiers were a little distracted, but not for long. The guards on duty were near the listening posts. The sound that was at first muffled coming from underground was now distinctly heard. Captain Krapivansky, apprehensive, walked through the trenches and reassured the soldiers. He promised that they would move from this position. He called Krivdin and asked permission to move.

The companies stayed in place. Soldiers were overwhelmed. Uneaten food was left in the pots. Brave Captain Krapivanky tried to joke around with the soldiers, but his usually appreciated jokes now went unnoticed. Soldiers stared at him with questioning gazes. He was powerless. Krivdin said to stay put.

"They're planning to bury us alive," Krapivansky told Krivdin.

"We can't go on like this. I am taking responsibility, and at night I am moving them to the reserve trenches," the captain announced to the battalion commander. I was always amazed by Krapivansky's brave talk with his superiors. I thought this captain wasn't afraid of anything or anybody.

Nighttime was approaching and with it, fear; soldiers waited. The Austrians didn't fire again. It was quiet the next day as well.

"We have to wait for the explosion," Krivdin communicated in a message. He wouldn't budge.

By Krapivansky's command, under cover of darkness, the soldiers were supposed to retreat to the reserve trenches. After dinner they didn't even lick their spoons. They drowsily tucked them into their boot tops, and if the spoon didn't obey, it was simply thrown out. Zhyk, the artillerymen's dog, fussed, jumped, and licked the soldiers' hands.

I ripped the blanket off the door of the dugout and tied it into a sack. I threw it over my shoulder and walked out. In the narrow walkway I noticed Sasha's familiar thin figure.

"Zina, Ivanov told me about everything. I'm sorry. Don't be mad. I know I offended you."

"I wasn't the one who was mad, it was you," I said.

I put the sack down and stood shifting my fur hat to the side.

"I came for you. Come with me, Zina. Captain Krapivansky is sending me to St. Petersburg. Answer me, Zina. I thought everything over. I want to marry you. Let's go, Zina. Don't you believe that even a soldier wants to be happy? And this would be a big, big happiness. So what do you say, sunshine?"

Snowy, murky-gray clouds hung over the trenches, and Sasha was talking to me about happiness, about sunshine.

"What do you need me for Sasha?" I asked.

"I'm telling you, I want to marry you. I'm not going to hide it from you. I love you, and that's that. Why are we still discussing this? Come with me, and we will live together."

I liked him. If I didn't see him for a while, I began to miss him. But be his wife? No! Where was I to go with him? I am not old enough, and what will they say at home, I thought.

"Sasha, I love you too, but to live with you and be your wife, that's something I can't do. My mother and father wouldn't want to give me away to you. I won't go with you, but I do love you."

Sasha responded, saying:

"You said it yourself, if you're going to love, then love for real; what now, you aren't brave enough or am I not good enough for you? You don't want to, Zina? I told you before you are a stranger to me, and I will tell you again, you are still a stranger to me. We are following different paths. I thought you were a different kind of girl since you went to war. I thought you stopped with this girl stuff, but I guess I was wrong. Well, good-bye. I'm not going to force you. It's your choice. Here is my picture and good-bye."

Sasha took a picture from his pocket, wiped it with a handkerchief, and gave it to me. He moved his hat to the side, so that his blonde hair was showing. He fixed the shoulder strap of his bag, said farewell to me with a long kiss, and went on. He looked back. My heart jumped in my chest. I wanted to run after him and stop him.

"Sasha, Sasha!" But I didn't yell it. I whispered it, and my timid call froze. I didn't call Sasha anymore. I picked up my sack and walked to the company.

〉〉〉

Lance Corporal Yeriga sang a song with the accompaniment of a three-stringed balalaika, swinging his head from side to side:

Not this one, then that one
Not this one, then that one
They spoke of war
A month
Or two
Not more—a few
Peace will come
The dark night will pass
The bright sun will rise
The German shoots the dugouts
Blood will soak the ground
Look, brothers, he is dead
And this one lies here wounded
But the officials with their heads held high
Speak of the end of the war
Not this one, then that one
Not this one, then that one
They spoke of war . . .

He sang his song over and over, and only when an officer arrived did he stop.

Yeriga, who always had his belt tightened to the very last loop, pulled on his short shirt, and watching the officer with his beady eyes, listened to the news. The officer talked about a cavalry regiment that refused to attack. The soldiers were on strike and didn't want to go, for the sixth time, to higher ground for an attack. There had been a lot of losses, and we heard stories about the never-ending artillery fire causing deafness.

Soldiers walked on snow-covered ground covered with corpses, and now there was an order to take the enemy's positions.

By nighttime the news was confirmed. The Stavropolsky and Krimsky regiments had to help the cavalry.

)))

At midnight we were relieved from our positions. The regiment was posted behind the village. A group of military policemen followed the rear guard. During the march the "Rashpils" arrested three cavalrymen who cheered up the tired with curses. The soldiers' feet were all wrapped up, and they couldn't walk anymore. The policemen didn't let them stop and poked them with their sticks. On the way we met hurried cavalrymen. One of them said: "Don't go there; they're leading you to your deaths." The infantry walked on, wincing. The military policemen caught deserters and beat them with rifles.

We made one long rest stop. The Stavropolsky Regiment walked thirty versts. People went without hot food, and they knew that soon they would have to fight in a battle. We scouts met two injured infantrymen along our way. One of them explained:

"We attacked and attacked, and now there are a hundred-something people left in the regiment. This is the sixth time we are going up to higher ground. Some of the guys are starting to desert us. They couldn't take it anymore, and everyone went in different directions. Then the cavalry refused to attack and ran. They say that a lot of our men have been caught deserting. It's horrible. Yesterday they beat up one deserter so badly it was scary. If there weren't so many of us that were injured, we wouldn't let them torture the others. Stepan Deryagin bled under the hands of the kind sirs."

The wounded took a smoke from us, and leaning on each other, walked off on the snowy field.

)))

The new trenches were tight fitting. There wasn't one good dugout here. Even I had to bend over to walk into our new homes. Trofim and I found an asylum. In the middle of the floor there stood some kind of broken box, and in the corner there was a pile of snow. The snow fell through a hole in the roof, and there was a log that came down low above our heads.

"We reached the winter housing, but it isn't any nicer here. It would be nice to go home right now and into a bed," Trofim said, shaking his head.

We sat down on the uncovered cot. Everyone was overwhelmed by the march and sitting in these trenches. The murky, hot, disgusting soup brought by the commissary man warmed us a little. We were falling asleep sitting up.

⟩⟩⟩

The ground shook. There was an echo with a scary, deafening howl.

"Something blew up!" someone said.

"Oh God, what is it now?" asked Trofim, who started making crosses on his chest.

Everyone ran out of the communications trench. Krivdin darted past us and said: "There was an explosion in the Twelfth Division."

Yeriga ran after him and asked: "Where? Who did it blow up?"

"They blew up our neighbors. We have to wait for an attack of the enemy or prepare for a counterattack."

The machine guns fired again. All over the front lines there was rapid fire. The artillery fire against us got stronger. The telephone operator ran past us. Klimich grabbed him by the sleeve and said: "Tell me what you know. Why is everyone so worried? There is no sense in this. Are they behind us or in front of us?"

"Our Twelfth Division sappers blew up the Austrians, and they are all in panic over there, trying to run away," the telephone operator answered.

"Thank God! We will be drinking tea with cookies in the morning!" And wrapping himself up in his old, gray scarf, Trofim wiped his mouth and crossed his chest.

No one even would have thought that at the same time, on the other side of the battlefield, our sappers were digging through the Austrian positions. No one expected to get to the warm Austrian barracks so soon. In the morning troops from the Stavropolsky and Krimsky regiments occupied four lines of Austrian trenches comfortably and without any losses.

Chereshenko twirled his mustache and smiled, commenting: "This is a sight! It's electricity on the front lines! Just like in our nobleman's factory. As soon as you turn it on, it sparkles like in a theater; it's beautiful. Those Austrians! It's a shame to kill such smart people."

Chereshenko kept turning the switch, marveling at the Austrian masteries. He said: "Did you see how they carried the ammunition in? Look here. They brought them on these little wagons. Oh holy mother of God, look, guys, they have a hanging washstand."

Trofim walked over to the washstand. Right next to it there was a clean towel hanging.

CHAPTER 10

There is a time lapse. It is winter, December 1916, in captured Austrian trenches. There is discussion about activists and discontent among troops about affairs in Russia under the czar. Zina receives an award for heroism, the St. George Cross, and decides to return home and visit her family.

The wind swept across the trenches and quieted down. There was smoke from the field kitchens above the Austrian lines. Their batteries were silent.

Winter arrived; everyone was trying to keep warm in the trenches. The soldiers split logs and lit fires in the twilight to keep warm. The officers had small metal stoves going.

We were given new sheepskin hats and bashliks. I really liked this new headgear and putting on the hat, I wrapped myself in the bashlik and looked at myself in the mirror. My face was even more tan and weathered from the constant marches. It was hot in the dugout, but I didn't want to take it off. I sat down and put my chin on my knees.

"I got a letter from Nastya. She says if necessary, she will come fight and be like Zina. She pays her respects to you. You hear?" asked Ivanov. He stood next to me, and on this bright winter day his voice didn't sound gloomy. Trofim was throwing wood into the fire and poking it with a bayonet. Yeriga tapped his foot and flicked his belt buckle, singing:

We sat in the dugouts
Went crazy from the lice
But the general came
He smacked us around
For no reason
That our insides hurt
We tell the platoon leader
Look
Wipe your tears away
He didn't understand the insult and beat us up

Trofim, smacking his lips, taking the cigarette out of his mouth, blew smoke and stared at Yeriga, commenting: "Listen to me, pal, your thoughts are like poisonous mushrooms growing after the rain. Get them out of your head."

"You, Trofim, are a serious guy, no joking around. I can't agree with you, so don't get mad at me. I'm going to be honest with you. You have no comprehension of God or loyalty to our government. You have too much faith, and you have too little intelligence," Yeriga replied.

Trofim answered: "What am I going to argue with you for? You are the smart one, no questions. The czar is the chosen one by God, and Russia is under his command and without . . ."

"The chosen one? Trofim, what's with you? What chosen one? You and me and the czar, we are all made of the same thing. Should I tell you whose folly it is that makes all our women and girls cry? My sister Katerina sent me a letter saying they took away our cow. It was our only cow. When I read her letter my hands shook, but I can't do anything from here. Zina, stop trying to be a lady. Go chop up some wood and tell them to give you a new hat. Your nose sticks out from under this one," Yeriga remarked.

Klimich shrugged his shoulders and walked back and forth, nervously brushing his orange beard with a broken comb.

"Let it go, Klimich! Big deal your daughter is getting married. It's time, the years are passing by. Why wait? I understand you are sad that they will have the wedding without you," Trofim added.

"You are saying this for no reason, Trofim. I know it's her time. I won't argue with that. But it's who she will marry that bothers me. He is the brother of Nikolai Fetikhin, a widower with three kids. He drinks night and day, and beat his late wife to death, and she was pregnant with a baby. Why do you speak like that when you don't know what's really going on? My Olenka is a beautiful girl. There's no one prettier! Oh boy, it's a shame," Klimich complained.

"Don't be upset, Klimich, sleep, the sorrow will pass. You can't do anything from over here anyway. They are far from us. Oh, how far they are, God forgive me, I am sinful," said Trofim.

"You are still crossing your chest, Trofim? So does it help?" asked Ivanov.

"Who knows, maybe it does help," he answered.

"I don't think it does much for you," commented Ivanov.

"We know you doubt God, Ivanov, we know," responded Trofim.

"He doubts the czar too," whispered Yeriga, who laughed merrily. He has such a contagious laugh that I laughed too.

"The czar, he is the blessed one, and all of Russia is under his command," Trofim added.

"The blessed one, are you serious, Trofim? You and I we are all made from the same dough, just like the czar along with his ministers. They aren't blessed, people moan from their mischief. Didn't you know that?" asked Yeriga.

"I know, I know, and David Markovitch told us many times. But still you doubt it," replied Trofim.

Again Yeriga and I laughed loudly.

"Be quiet, you two. God forbid we are heard," warned Trofim, stopping us.

Ivanov, smiling, looked at Trofim and then with resentment said:

"They confused all the men. Didn't they send us to protect their interests? They take away a man's land. Why does my Nastya stand at a working bench for twelve hours? She's poverty-stricken, and now has no strength. She writes to me, leave the war, we have to look out for ourselves. You think this isn't enough, Trofim, even though my wife started saying it? They can't make it over there. Do you understand?

Get that in your head, Trofim. As if you don't know what the rich do to the common people? Look a bit further."

"Maybe that is so, don't leave," replied Trofim.

"I will go, it's time. Good-bye for now," Ivanov answered.

Ivanov left. Everyone sat silent, nobody laughed any longer.

)))

I could barely chop the wood; I didn't have enough strength. I went to my platoon commander. I met a soldier on my way. He carried a pink bag under his arm and said to me: "Go tell the guys, Zina, the presents came, and we already got ours. It's all shit, but it's good enough to bet on."

I ran to the dugout with my heels striking against the hard ground. Chereshenko and Zaporozhets were visiting.

Chereshenko said: "You're late, I already told them, look at the mirror I got. I don't need it. Zina, if you get tobacco, exchange it with me."

He handed me a mirror, on the back of which was depicted the Czarina Alexandra. Klimich opened a box and said: "Here, Zina, the lollipops are good." Chereshenko laughed loudly, examining the presents and added: "Guys, what's the deal with this? I got a belt all nicely rolled up. Too bad Sasha isn't here. He likes this kind of stuff. It's not like there are any parties in the trenches, I would have nowhere to wear it." We sat there looking at the presents and making exchanges.

)))

The Stavropolsky Regiment relieved the Yakytsky Regiment. The days were unbearably cold. Many soldiers were sent to the rear lines with terrible gangrene caused by the frostbite. The brutally cold of winter 1916 didn't spare a soul.

At sunrise Trofim and I went on guard duty. The snow was falling.

"We've come to relieve you, get up," said Trofim, as he pushed the soldier on duty. The gray figure leaning against the wall had his head bent, and his dark beard rested on his chest. His hands were at his sides. One of his gloves was lying next to him on the ground.

"Get up, brother, we are relieving you," he repeated and bent over the soldier again. The gray figure didn't answer. Trofim got near the guard's ear and yelled: "We are relieving you! Wake up, brother!" Silence. All of a sudden Trofim grabbed my hand and squeezed it tightly, saying: "Zina, Zinochka, the snow isn't melting on him. He's dead. Oh God, he's dead." The guard didn't wake up to tell his dream to his friends.

Trofim picked up the glove and tried it on; it fit. He took the other one off the frozen fingers and shook them, saying: "I need it, I am sorry. Forgive me God, for I have sinned!"

Later the hospital attendants came. Groaning, they picked up the heavy, gray, frozen figure. The snow didn't melt in his deep wrinkles. His face was frozen in an eternal sleep. His knees wouldn't straighten either. On that spot where the guard fell asleep, there was his tobacco pouch still lying there and next to it lay a cigarette butt.

)))

When we came back there was nowhere to sit in our dugout. It was filled with soldiers. I walked up to the fire to warm my hands, and the tips of my fingers felt like they were burning. The soldiers were loud, each one interrupting the other. One commented: "Brothers, he told us that the regiment was sent to the reserve lines, and the activists were arrested. They will make an investigation. The main activist, they say, was a company secretary." Another soldier added: "Do you know what Gavrilka said? He came from St. Petersburg, and he said that the czar and czarina have a new priest who is in charge." The soldiers were buzzing like bees. I walked out of the dugout. Not too far from me stood a group of communications technicians who buzzed about something as well.

)))

The battle for Hill 367 had been raging for two days. The wounded lay all over the ruined huts and barns. The doctors, male nurses, and other help didn't have enough time to apply or reapply bandages. Many of the wounded were sent back without new bandages. There were many incidents where the soldiers fighting on the front lines had bandages applied by inadequately trained personnel. Thinking that the wound "burned," they would put the wrong black side of the bandage on a fresh wound, which caused numerous infections. It was hard to reteach the nurses, and even though the doctors would correct them, it continued to be done. Despite the repeated requests from the doctors, they continued this practice.

The fat, clumsy male nurse, Nayumich, put a wad of gauze into the bloody eye of a wounded soldier with his short, fat fingers. The soldier's tears mixed with drops of blood and trickled down his face to his torn collar. Surgeon Morozov finished the operation.

A warrant officer, opening his mouth wide, took a huge gulp of air. The cotton, with strong-smelling medicine on it, pressed against his nose again. He was starting to doze off. They covered the soldier, put him on the stretcher, and carried him to the surgeon at the other side of the hut.

It looked as if they cut a huge piece of meat from Bashmakin's shoulder blade with a sharp knife. They applied a few layers of bandage, but the blood seeped through anyway.

"Send him to the mobile hospital," a voice directed. The male nurse picked up the soldier with his strong hands and put him on a stretcher. A new group of wounded soldiers just arriving filled the place with wild screams.

The skinny, small, meek artillery sergeant, Kyzka, wounded in the groin, was in a deep sleep. Dr. DeMorrey took off his glasses. He fogged the glasses with his breath, and then worked on wiping them with his handkerchief. Putting his hands behind his back, he leaned over the wounded. Near Kyzka's wound, lice sucked on the blood on his fat stomach. The blood was almost all dry, and his hair was stuck together. A sharp edge of a shell fragment was sticking out.

"The wound is nothing, wake him up," DeMorrey said to the male nurse. The soldier was awakened. Kyzka's blue eyes stared up at the doctor.

"Am I going home?" Kyzka asked.

"Maybe you will, but for now you are going to the hospital, and it won't be more than a month," DeMorrey replied.

"I want to go home," Kyzka said.

Seeing the scalpel in the doctor's hands, Kyzka sat up. His innocent, blue eyes stared at the shiny instrument and then at the wound. He saw the lice. He cried like a baby, saying: "Oh my God, mother of mercy, they're everywhere! How can I get away from them? They're eating at my wound, those damned . . ." He kept crying and crying until he couldn't breathe.

They carried in a soldier with a beard and put him on the table. They opened up his coat. The broken-down hut was filled with a sickening smell. They turned him over to the side and cut his trousers. On his rear there was a gashing wound. Blood was mixed with a yellow mass. They cleaned his wound from a little tub that the nurse brought. A nurse carried a needle with ammonium, and as he stuck it into the soldier, he let out a cry of agony.

A high-cheek-boned Tatar with narrow eyes stood in line waiting to be bandaged. They unwrapped Ibrahim Axmedov's wounded hand. It was black and badly burnt. A nurse cleaned around the wound with peroxide.

"You wounded yourself?" asked DeMorrey, laughing. The doctor, looking at the wound and running his hand over his clean-shaven face, teased the soldier, asking: "Did it shoot itself? Did it shoot itself?" The nurse was already writing something down in a notebook.

"Didn't you take an oath of allegiance? Forgot who you are serving?" growled Nayumich. With a small, thin voice Axmedov answered, staring at the tip of the doctor's nose: "I served in barracks. I served in the trenches. I need to go to Kazan."

The young Tatar smiled guiltily and looked at DeMorrey questioningly. He stared at the doctor and then at the surrounding soldiers. Ibrahim Axmedov didn't know about the severe punishment for those with self-inflicted wounds. There was an order that those who inflict self-injury will be punished with fifty lashes with a whip, and a second attempt would be punished by a court-martial. He hadn't yet seen the scary military policeman Dybelo, who supervised the punishments. He looked at his newly wrapped bandage, and turning his hand like a marionette, he smiled. That winter month there were more and more cases of self-inflicted injuries.

)))

We awaited the arrival of the Romanians in the trenches. Our artillery discovered Austrian scouts on the customs building and kept firing at it nonstop. A few of our shells fell short and hit the Romanians. The next day the Romanians demanded an explanation.

The officers from the headquarters prepared for the meeting. Captain Melnikov's cigarette box was shining and gleaming in the sunlight. The officers' boots were shining too. The officers walked through the trenches, occasionally looking out. Finally we sighted a group of Romanians walking towards our trenches. They walked with an especially careful manner in their shining, black boots. Their servants walked behind them carrying little leather briefcases.

After the greetings, our artillery officers started explaining and apologizing for the accidental fire that fell short. The Romanians, all flushed, were telling our artillery officers something. After spending half an hour in the battalion commander's dugout, everyone walked out again.

The Romanians shook the hands of the Russian officers, and looking obviously calm and content, were on their way back to their border. Their servants walking behind them would occasionally run up to them in answer to their shouts, and opening their briefcases, would take out appetizing oranges and give it to their officers. Soldiers of our battalion, crawling on the ground, began to pick up the orange peels that the Romanians left.

)))

I kept seeing artilleryman Ivanov more often among the soldiers. He looked gloomy. His eyes looked worried. One time he said to me: "Soon Sasha will come back. He is needed here now."

"What about me?" I asked.

Ivanov moved me gently. He quickly went to the rest of the company. I couldn't resist and ran after him. He spoke almost in a whisper: "Which one of you doesn't get it yet?"

"Well, you told us about the enemy among us, are you really saying that the German or the Austrian or the Frenchman isn't our enemy?" someone asked.

"The Germans have rich folk too, they are our enemies. It wouldn't matter who won now, the Russians, the Germans, or the Austrians. The goal is to have peace as soon as possible. Do you understand?" Ivanov asked.

"That's right. But will they really give us more land at the end of the war?" a voice responded.

"We have to win the land back ourselves from the landlords. Right now the most important thing is peace," replied Ivanov.

"Quiet," someone said.

Bashmakin opened the door. There was the weak noise of steps coming from the communications trench.

"Guys, separate! Lieutenant Zambor is walking around the trenches," warned one of the soldiers. In a hurry, Yeriga knocked over a cauldron of burnt oatmeal.

"He can go to hell. Quiet, guys. Disperse slowly," Ivanov warned.

)))

The December days became more severe. Soldiers got frostbite. They called me to the regimental headquarters. On the way to the village of Zavarovtsi, I met a few artillerymen from the Fourth Battery who said: "Volunteer, come visit us."

I swerved off the road and followed a narrow path to the battery. The soldiers greeted me and fed me dinner. They showed me an artillery piece and explained how it worked. I left them late that night.

In the morning, at regimental headquarters, the regimental adjutant opened an envelope and pulled out a St. George Cross of the fourth degree, which he pinned onto my coat.[1]

"This is for showing bravery in battle near the village of Simki," he said.

I don't remember leaving the headquarters, but I ran to my company as fast as I could. I still heard the words of the adjutant, "for the bravery . . ." It was freezing outside, but I was hot. I remember looking at the medal gleaming in the sun while holding it steady with one arm.

In the communications trench I almost knocked over Ivanov, who saw my cross, but didn't say anything. I felt the January cold again. My happiness cooled off. It would be nice if Ivanov congratulated me, but he left. And Sasha? Trofim? They don't have a cross; Klimich has two, Chereshenko has one, but recently he said: "What the hell do I deserve this for? To hell with them! I fought against my peasant brother!"

I didn't run anymore. I walked with the feeling of annoyance and bitterness.

I tripped and fell at the door of our dugout. I looked around to see if anyone saw, but the fall hurt me, and my leg immediately began to hurt. I imagined a scene from my childhood. It was during my transition from first to second grade. My mother promised to fulfill my wish, to buy me a black doll, but only if I went to the next grade without retaking any tests. Every day I walked past the toy store. In the window display there was the beautiful black doll. She was in a red dress with white polka dots. On that memorable day, when on my report card it said, necessary to retake test for arithmetic, I walked past the same display. The black doll stood there showing off as usual. At home my mother asked me: "Did you make it?" I lied to her and said: "Without any reexaminations." And when she asked to see my report card, I told her we didn't get them yet. I had only one wish, to have that black doll. I was holding her tight in my arms by the evening.

The next day my mother bumped into my arithmetic teacher and found out the truth. That day, when I sat in the nursery and brushed the untamable hair of my new doll, I was called into my father's office. There were three chairs. I was put on them, my clothes pulled off and my naked body was whipped. Later there was no black doll in my room. She was put back into the box and never given back to me. This kind of punishment had a great effect on me. In those hours I felt very much alone, and besides the physical pain, I seemed funny and pitiful. Ever since then, I was always afraid of looking funny.

)))

In the dugout Yeriga threw his balalaika, and his little eyes were fixed on my St. George Cross.

"Look! Zina got a cross! It's probably for being a scout, right when you carried one of those important messages, right?" Yeriga asked.

"You should probably take a trip home now, Zina. But if you go, you wouldn't come back, right?" questioned Trofim.

I didn't care anymore. I hid the hanging cross in my pocket.

Yeriga gave me a German field bag. He convinced me to visit home, saying: "Don't be scared, they will give you documents, and as soon as you want, you can return back to us. We will all be going home soon anyway. You will see."

All of a sudden something pulled me home. I wanted to say so much to them, and I wanted to let them see what I've become. All night I dreamed of our house, of my mother, my father, Valya, and our old nanny, Alekseevna.

In the morning I went to the battalion commander and told him of my wishes. I dodged every bullet that day and fell on the ground at the sound of every shell. I felt like it was all aimed at me.

CHAPTER 11

Zina returns home to visit her family in December 1916 and suffers growing anguish over the effect of the war on the common Russian people. She has embraced revolutionary ideals and decides to forsake the wishes of her family to remain home and instead return back to the front to help end the war for the benefit of the common people.

Sitting on the train, I didn't let go of my bag even for a minute, and I kept looking at all of the documents in it. It had my ticket, my notice of permission to leave the army, my award letter, and my authorization to get back into the army.

I am going home. I started walking to the first class section at Zhmerynka station.[1] I was stopped at the doors by a security guard saying: "Soldiers aren't supposed to go here, go to third class."

"I am coming from the front lines," I stated.

"You aren't supposed to be here, move," said some officer, as he pushed me.

I wanted to go into the first class section so badly, so everyone could see that I was a girl fighting in the war. But I was rudely denied entrance, and they didn't care whether I came from the front lines or not. I looked at the security guard surprised and turned around. A general was nearing the doors. On his shoulders was a coat with red lining.[2]

"Let the volunteer through, he's a George Cross winner!" ordered the general.

The security guard stepped aside, stroking his beard.

"Please, please go right ahead. Sorry!" he said, letting me through into the first class waiting room.

There, walking to a table, I sat down on a chair. The colonel sitting across from me got up and said: "If you are going to sit at the senior commanders table, you have to ask permission. Do you have an ID?"

I opened my bag and importantly stretched out my documents to him.

"It's very nice to meet you, which is rare. Where are you off to?" he asked.

He asked me so many questions I barely had time to answer each one. Finally it was the soft low voice of the conductor: "Second call, Odessa—Moscow!"—that cut off the colonel's question. I got up hurriedly and jumped onto the platform, running towards my train.

In Bryansk the conductor informed everyone of the long stop here.[3] Instead of the usual forty minutes, the train was stopped for twenty-four hours. In the third class waiting room the soldiers sat leaning on one another. A woman with a baby stood by the wall with the garbage can. Seeing me, she got up. In broken Russian she said to me: "Listen, boy, maybe you are coming from the army. Did you see my Nikolai there? He was in the infantry. He wrote home that he is going to take leave. Eight weeks have passed already, and he still hasn't come home. I've been running around all of the train stations looking for him, but he isn't here. He disappeared here."

The woman cried, and shaking her head kept repeating: "Nikolai isn't here, he isn't here! He disappeared! That's it!"

Many trains blocked the way. Sticking their heads out of the medical train, the nurses invited me to join them. Two of them, dark brunettes always laughing, lunged at me and started kissing me. They treated me to candy and offered me wine. The third one, they called her Sophia Garina, looked at me with sad, exhausted eyes. She pulled me by the hand, and we went out into the corridor where I heard:

"Tell me the truth, are the people on the front lines kinder than here? How can I get there? I can't stay here. Everyone is always drinking. It's disgusting. I'm sick of it! And it's so hard to be the only one fighting it.

The way they look at us nurses—Oh it's a nurse—that means they can do anything they want with us. It's hard to keep your reputation here. I've been in three infirmaries near the front lines, and it's the same thing everywhere. I can't leave this job. At home my parents are old and sick, and my father has a small pension. My family will starve. As soon as you defend yourself, they pick on you. A couple of days ago they almost fired me. I slapped an officer because he went too far. He filled his mouth with cognac and spit it at me, and then he tried to kiss me. He kept saying, 'kiss me, kiss me.' I can't be here anymore! I can't!"

A nurse walking past us sang:

Live life while you can
And sing song while you can
Because in life
We live only once . . .

Sister Garina wrote down her address and stuck the note in my hand.

Saying farewell to them, I went on walking along the medical train. Male nurses in white coats carried off wounded soldiers.

Heavily drunk and barely moving their feet, a military police captain with a young lieutenant walked over to the medical train. Out of one of the train cars, with the help of a nurse, a soldier walked on crutches. The officers walking stopped right next to him, and one with a drunk voice said: "Blew your legs off? Poor soldier! So you are going to get fired legally? Why do you put your head down?" And he pulled the soldier's nose up with full force. The soldier's eyes filled up with tears from the pain.

The officers, held up for a moment by the lieutenant, walked a few steps farther and walked back by a wounded German officer. A German lieutenant was wounded in the chest, and his breathing sounded like a whistle escaping from his lungs. The captain fell back as if broken, he was so drunk. He bent over the German shouting: "He's snoring, that pig!" And he sharply kicked the German.

All of a sudden the wounded German jumped up, leaving a big bloody stain on the stretcher's linen. His eyes burned with fever. His pale face twitched with convulsions. He got up despite his wounds, straightened his back, and with a proud German march, walked past the drunken officers.

The nurses with the stretchers winced and looked at the drunken officers, quietly saying: "Dogs, even they won't touch someone when they're down." They looked at the drunken officers and with lost expressions on their faces, followed the German lieutenant. The drunken captain and lieutenant, turning to each other, laughed unpleasantly and headed towards the train car where loud singing was coming from the nurses.

Walking along the platform for the hundredth time, I was attracting the attention of passersby. I was stopped more than once. People were asking what regiment I was with, what was my age, and they looked at my medal.

〉〉〉

The night dragged on. The train began to move very early. The tracks were covered with snow. People were still asleep in the villages. There were a few dim lights in the cottages.

In the morning our train left. I was annoying the conductor with all my questions of when we were going to get to Kazan. Changing in the evening, I found the note from Sister Garina. She wrote in her small handwriting:

Don't be surprised at my wish to go to the front lines. I was infected with a terrible disease. I'm going to die. I don't want to live like this, and I don't have it in me to kill myself. When I get killed at war, the money will go to my elderly parents.

〉〉〉

There was a whistle-stop. A sleepy woman in a fur coat raised a faded green flag, letting the train go. A girl was pulling on her skirt. A black puppy indignantly threw the snow to the side with its back paws. Pushing each other, the frozen sunflowers swayed. From my window I could see the last car and the woman. The woman lazily lowered the flag and walked away to the little, lonely booth standing in the midst of the snow.

We went along the empty village roads. The rural cottages disappeared behind the hills. The little spruce trees shook, frightened by the train. The sun broke through the winter fog, illuminating the new day with a happy pink color. The train stopped. I jumped out onto the station of my beloved Kazan.

An old, white horse with brown spots pulled me along to the Admiralty district. I felt like I would never get home. The driver, waving his whip, looked back at me and said:

"I know your mother; I've gone to the city with her plenty of times. And I knew your dead brother, may he rest in peace. He used to go to school with my Vanya. Demyan Alekseevitch, the geography teacher, helped get my Vanya free admission. He was very dedicated to learning. Stay, you restless creature! My son is still in school. He has a talent for learning. Well, here we are; this is where the Kramskys live."

I searched in my bag for the little, knotted handkerchief. I was so anxious to see my family that my hands shook. I kept my silver coins in the handkerchief that I won in the trenches when we played heads and tails. I paid the driver and jumped out. I stood on the porch for a long time, not confident enough to ring the bell. Finally I stood on my tiptoes and rang the bell. I heard Valya's familiar footsteps running down the stairs.

"Who is it?"

"Valya, open it! It's family."

Without kissing or hugging me, my sister ran through the corridor shouting: "Mama! Zina came back!" There was a second of silence and then my sister's voice again: "Hurry up, Zina came back!"

My mother didn't let me out of her embrace, hugging me closely. She felt my hair, my face and hugged me again. My father kissed me many times. Valya, jumping up and down in one spot, screamed: "Hooray! Zina's back! Our Zina is such a hero! Such a hero! Mama let her go, seriously, she isn't leaving anymore."

In a minute I was sitting in the kitchen, and our nanny had tears streaming down her face and was petting my head saying: "Zinochka, why did you leave me, I'm so old, and the times are so rough. My little lady became a soldier! My dead Ulyanich told such stories about war with Turkey. You weren't scared to get captured by the Germans?"

"Alekseevnushka, I will tell you about everything. I will," I said.

My father walked from corner to corner of the room smoking his pipe. Toby, our old dog, smelled me for a long time and licked my hands, whining and barking, and then he finally calmed down and lay near my feet.

"Sit, please, sit," Mother said, as she begged father not to walk around. She moved closer to me and hugged me again.

"Don't walk around," she said to him again. Maybe she wanted to hear the beating of my heart, and father's footsteps were interrupting.

"I missed you, my dear," said my father. He bent over and fixed my cross.

"Zina, what is the cross for?" asked Valya, who was curious. And then she said: "Zina, look how many birds I have. Look, I will show you all of them. This is Yasha, this is the bullfinch Spiridon, and this is the bluebird Ganka."

It was very quiet at home and so, so warm. Overwhelmed by the road and nurtured by my mother, I fell asleep in my warm, soft bed that night.

The next day after visiting all our friends, my sister and I were coming home, and not too far from the house we were harassed by a group of boys. Seeing me, they approached us and stuck out their tongues and made every kind of face possible. One of the teenagers, looking at my medal, cursed at me. I was upset and annoyed, and running up to the tall blond boy, I attacked him. My unexpected burst and powerful kicks amazed the boys. The rest of them ran up to the blond one and started hitting him too, which Valya and I found completely unexpected. He jumped away from us and ignoring his defeat, yelled: "Yeah, right! A soldier with breasts!"

The boys touched my medal, and one of them, very much concerned, fixed my coat. We talked peacefully, and then taking Valya's hand, we walked away. Turning around one last time, I held up my fist up to them.

At home, my sister told my father the whole story, overemphasizing and wildly gesturing. Alekseevnushka listened with her mouth open the whole time. I just lay on the couch and whistled.

Every evening I sat by the stove surrounded by my family. I didn't even notice how much I was telling them about life on the front lines.

Valya listened with her big, pretty, gray eyes wide open. My mother stared at me, and the old nanny kept wiping her tears.

Interrupting me occasionally, my father would ask me: "I trust you are not going back anymore?"

)))

The house smelled of holiday gingerbread and cake. Everyone's pre-holiday jitters made me get up quickly and get dressed. My father was doing something with a big wooden box in the hall. Moving my mother over slightly, he was looking for something at the very bottom. The aroma of vanilla, cinnamon, and tobacco smoke from my father's pipe reminded me of General Mitchvolodov. He smelled just as gingery.

"It's here! I found it! I found it! said my father. He pulled out a long fencing foil and held it up with shaking hands. My mother walked past him with his frock coat.

In a few minutes my father walked into the room stroking his beard and wearing his coat and hobnail boots that made noise as he walked. "All right, Zinochka, make your old father happy, let's go to church," he said. I put on my jacket that was given to me as a present by Akylka, brushing the fur on it, and twirled in front of the mirror a few times. Father bent over and fixed my cross, wiping it with a handkerchief, and I walked out of the house with him.

)))

A soldier made his way to the church, tapping on the stone with his crutches. Two old ladies in velvet, wearing hats with violets that barely covered their heads, walked out of the church. Making little crosses on their chests, they almost fainted seeing me, remarking: "Mademoiselle Kramskaya—a soldier!"

I laughed out loud. My father looked at me sternly. The beggars between us moved away, and surprised, they put down their hands and whispered.

My father walked forward in church to be closer to the front. Everyone bowed for the soldiers killed in the war. The chorus was singing, "Good gracious God." The priest walked past us swinging the thurible and waving the incense before the icons. He slanted his eyes at me and slowed down a little.

Leaning towards my father, I whispered: "Let's go. I'm sick of this place. I want to go home."

"Let's wait a bit more, daughter," said my father, getting up from his knees. He got closer to me. I smelled the tobacco from his clothes. Like never before, all of a sudden I felt claustrophobic. The dim lights, the crowded room, everybody praying, it was too much. I pulled my father by the sleeve and went in the direction of the exit. My father, unhappy, mumbled something.

Unwilling, he walked out of the church. At the door we met the local museum's director, old Phillip Karlovich Glin, who remarked: "Have you heard, Leonid Konstantinovich, that things aren't going well in St. Petersburg? Before going off to the war, a few military units went on strike. They screamed, 'stop the war.' They attempted to assassinate Rasputin.[4] Can you believe what is going on?!" And turning to the church, he started crossing his chest, repeating: "God help and forgive us! God help and forgive us!" They spoke a bit about a mammoth bone that was recently found, and Glin said good-bye. My father walked silently.

I met our caretaker, Peter Semenovitch, at the gate. He looked even older than I remembered. I greeted him, shaking his hand.

"Did your Mitya come back?"

"No. You don't return from there," he replied.

"Come visit us. Would you like to come now?" I asked. The caretaker looked half-heartedly at my father.

"I'll come later," he said.

"Zina, I am waiting for you. Let's go," urged father.

"I'll come to you. We will talk. I will tell you how it is over there," I said.

My tooth hurt badly. My father called the cab driver, and we got into a carriage and went to the doctor. At the end of Gruzinskaya Street we had to get out and walk. It was noisy. A crowd of people walked on the way to the Arskom field surrounded by wardens. Some people were wrapped in gray robes, all huddled from the cold, and others opened up their coats and wiped the sweat from their foreheads, as if it were from a hot July day. Many looked about frightened at people walking past, looking for someone. Still some cried like children or laughed unnaturally. The eyes of a young woman gleamed, and her cheeks were inflamed. Her face was gentle and smiling. She held tightly onto a bundle of rags. "Sleep, sleep, my dear . . ." Her velvety contralto song quietly poured forth.

It was a group of insane people evacuated from Warsaw to Kazan. Behind them, raving lunatics were driven in carriages with peeling paint. Occasionally there would be a hysterical scream coming from there. The crowd stopped, but their noise didn't. The lights of the psychiatric ward in the hospital were lit. The cast-iron doors opened, and the gray walls welcomed their new guests.

)))

The days that were at first happy and filled with love of my relatives were now long and boring. The silence of our house irritated me. Everything was the same here: the warm house, the purring of our cat, the dog running around, and my mother by the piano playing a sad waltz.

Everyone left; I was left alone in the house. The comfortable silence frightened me. Valya's birds scratched at their cages with their claws. The cat Peter purred and the old dog Toby snored. The pendulum calmly swung in the clock. All of a sudden I wanted to change everything, move the furniture, tear the flowers, and turn everything upside down. I jumped up from the couch, ran up to the clock, forcefully pushed the pendulum, threw up the curtains, woke up the cat, and ruffled up Toby. I pushed the rocking chair with my foot. I grabbed Valya's guitar, playing it like a balalaika. Toby barked, the cat raised its tail and jumped on the piano from which a bundle of old waltz music fell. The dog scattered them about. Everything was in motion.

"What's all this noise?" father asked. He fixed his glasses, walked up to the clock, and stopped it.

"The music notes fell, I'll pick them up," I said.

"I am free, let's talk. Tell me what it's like in the war. Did you meet your officers? Who commands your division? I read about the 19th Division," he said.

"General Mitchvolodov. I saw him once. I haven't seen other generals on the front lines," I answered.

"He probably has a lot of medals?" inquired father.

"I don't know," I said.

"Of course the soldiers have to go to battle. There are a lot of them," he replied.

"But the generals want this war, not the soldiers," I stated.

"What do you mean? What about their country and their motherland?" he asked.

"The people are getting poorer from this war and are not seeing anything good. Don't you know that the rich need this war? Don't you know that the Germans and the Austrians have rich people who force them to fight for their own gain?" I replied.

"Who drilled this nonsense into your head?" he asked.

"If you only saw everything," I responded.

"What's everything?" he said.

"Why does Lieutenant Zambor beat the soldiers?" I asked.

"They apparently are disobedient in some way. The soldiers, we heard, for example, only fight once the whip is cracked. Who will protect the country? Who is Lieutenant Zambor? You know him? He is probably a very brave officer," said my father.

"Zambor has a big estate near Kiev," I answered.

"Oh, he has to be a brave officer. Does he stand by a machine gun?" he asked.

"Yeriga stands by it and the others, but not him," I said.

"Who is Yeriga? That's not a very nice sounding last name," he said.

"Yeriga is my good friend," I said.

My father shrugged his shoulders and looked at me with disbelief. The doorbell rang in the hall. I opened the door. A civil servant, Ivan Spiridonovitch, walked in.

"How wonderful it is, your Zina, is a hero," he remarked.

"Adventure! Now I see that it's an adventure of the young, Ivan Spiridonovitch," said father angrily.

I shut the door behind him and left. I teased my father loudly and ran down the stairs saying: "Adventure! Adventure!"

The door opened. I heard Ivan Spiridonovitch say to my father: "Did you hear, Konstantine Konstantinovitch, that St. Petersburg is not calm. Those marching refuse to go to the front lines. Can you believe what is happening?"

"You didn't tell me the most important thing. What do they say about the war over there, is it going to be over soon? I can't wait for Vacya," father replied.

"Zina, Zinochka, your father is calling you!" shouted Ivan Spiridonovitch.

Alekseevnushka stood in the middle of the yard, and Valya waited for me on the porch.

"Where were you, with Peter Semenovitch?" asked father.

"You are friends with the caretaker? You haven't been with your mother, but you spend hours in the caretaker's lodge," he commented.

"There is no news from Vacya," he added.

"Who is Vacya?" I asked.

I looked at my father. I wanted to yell at him, yell so that the whole yard would be filled with my screams, so that he could finally understand the grief of old Peter Semenovitch.

At night, throwing myself on my bed, I confided in my mother: "Mother, I can't live like this anymore! I can't stay here. I'm with you, father, Valya, my friends, but you all don't understand anything. You are so close to me, yet so far away. You see, half of me is here, and the other half is there."

Crying loudly from despair because I couldn't figure out what had happened, I told my mother again: "I . . . I can't stay here. Mother, who am I? You have to understand, I cracked. I cracked, and there is no way to piece me back together!"

"Zinochka, my Zina, what are you saying?" my mother asked. "Oh God, what has happened to you? You are losing your mind. It must be a fever. I will call the doctor."

"I don't have a fever. I don't need a doctor. I am perfectly healthy. Mother, please understand!" I insisted.

Who am I really? I asked myself a thousand questions I couldn't answer, and my mother sat next to me pressing cold compresses I didn't need to my face. For a long time I couldn't fall asleep on the feather bed and soft pillows fluffed up by my mother. I picked my head up from a tear-soaked pillow in the morning.

)))

In the afternoon our parents had guests over. My sister and I barely had time to run to the door over and over. There was the old, prim head-mistress of the Rodinovsky Institute for noble girls, Madame Depreis, two officials and their wives, and a mathematics teacher. Then there was Valya's teacher, the black-haired student Innokenty.

Madame Depreis would look at me through her thick glasses every minute. Moving all around in her chair, she didn't stop expressing how appalled she was, saying: "Oh, Leonid Konstantinovich, your Zina used to be so quiet, and now your Zina is a soldier all of a sudden. After all, that's a bit shameless."

Madame Depreis put down her glasses and added: "She will not go to the war again. What kind of jokes are these, a lady in a soldier's fantasy."

"Youth, youth, adventure," said father, fixing his glasses and looking at me very unfriendly.

"What are you talking about, she's a hero," someone remarked.

I heard Alekseevnushka coming down the hall. Assistant District Attorney Valery Kasianovich Kunev ran into the room, without taking his coat off, and said: "Excuse me, I am here for only a minute. I have news! Rasputin was killed. And they say . . ."

"What?" Everyone started asking and talking all at once. Kunev whispered something in father's ear.

"Finally an end to the Russian ruler," said Innokenty, as he got up and walked out of the room.

"Such horror," whispered Madame Depreis. She took out a piece of paper and said: "Imagine, dearest, a few days ago they found this poem in the girls' room. I suspect the brother of this girl, he is a volunteer. Please read it." Father read:

In the capital, heels resound in the doors of the restaurant
But here in the trenches there is a howling of the devil

There the general is hugging a cutie
But here in the trenches a soldier curses his scabs

The ministers stuff their pockets
But here the soldiers wash their wounds with tears

In the parlors there are Rasputin's drunk parties
But here in the trenches everyone is overcome with lice

"Yes, my friends, that is free speech. Who knows what the youth is doing nowadays? The revolution has its sprouts everywhere," said the assistant district attorney, as he loudly blew his nose.

"Well, Valery Kasianovich, but not in my institute," responded Madame Depreis.

"I will be off now. I have a lot of things to do, you know!" Kunev said.

"Have some pancakes, Valery Kasianovich. It's not the religious holiday, but not far from it," mother forcefully offered.

"I'm sorry, I cannot stay, Lydia Arkadievna. I'm in such a state, so overwhelmed and flustered, I will run on," Kunev answered.

Alekseevnushka stood in the doorway, not coming in. "Zinochka, my love there is a soldier here asking about you."

The guests stared at me and then at my parents. Madame Depreis shuffled in her chair. I tripped over her chair, and my father yelled after me: "You didn't even apologize to the Madame."

Running to the kitchen, I froze. On the bench next to Alekseevnushka's bed, staring at his hands, sat the thin and aged Klimich, who said: "I am just stopping by, Zina. I got your address from Yeriga. I thought I might as well come by and meet your family. I was slightly injured, so I went home for a day or two. The doctor let me go, so I am going back to the front lines."

He stood there with a lost look on his face. He played with his fur hat. I jumped on him, hugging him, and asked him thousands of questions.

Standing behind me, Alekseevnushka couldn't stop herself: "What will your mother say? That is embarrassing. You should be ashamed, Zinochka."

I took off Klimich's coat, took him by the hand, and led him into the dining room.

"Mama, this is Vaciliy Klimich, my guest. Sit, Klimich," I said.

Vaciliy Klimich greeted my family members and shook hands with the guests. Madame Depreis stretched out two fingers to him, and I saw how she hid her fingers under the tablecloth, and carefully taking out a handkerchief wiped her hand. Valya moved the pancakes closer to Klimich. Silence settled in for a few minutes. My father smoked his pipe. Alekseevnushka stood in the doorway leaning on the wall. She folded her hands across her chest and tapped her large fingers. My father broke the silence: "Are you coming from the front lines or on your way there?"

"I am coming from home. Now I'm on my way back. I was wounded. We were with your daughter in the trenches under fire many times," Klimich said.

"What is the news from home? Tell us what they say in your village," my father asked.

Klimich responded: "Well, that it's all coming to the point where they refuse to fight. We are shedding blood against our brothers. But the upper class . . ."

"And you, soldier, you are going to war?" asked Madame Depreis, interrupting and humbly bowing her head.

"I am going to the front lines. We will end this war," Klimich replied.

"Tell me, is it true that Zinochka was really a scout under the German barbed wire?" Valya asked curiously.

"That is most certainly true, little lady. I'm not hiding a thing, and your sister has courage like no other. It was more than once that she crawled under barbed wire on her stomach," he answered.

Madame Depreis abruptly moved her chair, and the guests looked worried. Mother tried to convince her to stay longer, but the guests were getting ready to leave. Behind us I heard the quick patter of Alek-seevnushka's feet. Klimich and I were left alone.

"Zina, tomorrow evening I'm going. It's a tough time now, and I have to go to the front. The people are so poor. They have no more energy. Don't think about it, Zina, just come with me, and we will fight for them to end the war. We don't need it. Let the noblemen fight their own battles. Come with me, now is not the time to be in your mother's protection. I will come see you tomorrow, but right now thank you for the hospitality." And gently Klimich added: "Your sister is great, your mother is nice, but your father is a little gloomy."

"Klimich, stay with us, I will think about it and tell you tomorrow," I answered.

"Have some more tea," my father offered, returning with my mother.

"No thank you," Klimich replied. He got up and bidding good-bye to my parents, he walked out.

"I visited your daughter, and now it is time to go to sleep," he said.

Valya was trying to get Klimich to stay with us.

"No, I cannot, my countrymen are waiting for me," he said.

Klimich put on his coat, and Valya and I walked him to the door. Mother and father weren't there.

"You have such a long beard," Valya remarked.

"And you, miss, have such a long braid," smiled Klimich.

I walked outside, and Alekseevnushka pulled my hand: "Button up, you will catch a cold. The shaggy one flung the door open!"

"The old woman has an attitude," replied Klimich. "Go, Zina. Pack your things. We will go tomorrow. There's no need to think too long."

)))

That evening, my mother stayed up with me until late.

"Mother, I want to go back to the army," I said, not thinking for long.

"What are you saying, Zina! God forbid! These are restless times. You heard what they said. You will die there. Zina, tell me what do you need. What is it that you yearn for? Don't leave, my dear! Your father barely lived through your departure. This is going to be a big blow for him again. Don't do this! Have mercy for your father and me! Everybody knows we are on the verge of big things happening. Not today, then maybe tomorrow, there will be a major strike. Where are you going to go? You are going to die. You are going to die, Zina. You need to go to school, or you will not be educated. What will come of you then?"

"Don't plead with me, mother, I cannot stay here. I don't know what will happen to me, but I already told you I cannot stay here."

My mother hugged me, and I barely got her off me. She held on to me and cried. Everyone in the house got together. Alekseevnushka was splashing water on her, and my father and sister were running around putting cold packs on her heart.

Valya interjected: "You are mean, Zina. One thing is for sure . . ."

"I am not mean, Valya. You don't understand anything," I interrupted.

I spent long hours in my father's den. He was behind the door, calming down mother. They gave her pills, splashed her with water, and at those moments I didn't feel bad for her. Maybe this was bad, but those tears, my mother's tears that once used to touch me, now seemed so unnecessary, and this whole hysterical show she put on too. I had no sympathy towards my mother. I decided to go with Klimich.

I wanted to be alone with my thoughts. I got up off my bed and went into my father's office. I didn't have time to see mother. I felt like they all became so little, and I was older than all of them, and I was ashamed for my father, that he was being so little. He was so big and old at the same time and couldn't understand me. I will go. And all of a sudden I felt a wave of unbelievable happiness wash over me. I waited impatiently for the morning, and as soon as the sun began to rise, I got dressed and walked out into the garden.

Behind the fence I heard the creaking of sleds with firewood. With its pink glow, the sunrise was playfully reflected on the backs of the horses covered in frost. The strong winter air hurt my lungs and burned my cheeks. A Christmas tree with its branches hanging down was bent towards the ground. The old dog, limping, ran from tree to tree.

I returned home where everything was calm with sleep. Alekseevnushka snored in the kitchen. I came into my room, and without changing, I packed my things into a bag. I got ready for my departure. I was pulled by some force back to the regiment, there into that big family. "Hooray!" I yelled in a voice that was not my own. "Hooray, I am going to see you all again!"

)))

I walked passed Alekseevnushka in the kitchen. Everyone was silent at breakfast. Valya got up, fed the birds, and changed the water. Without looking each other in the eye, everyone got up and went to their own corners. The birds were noisy, not quieting down at all. Alekseevnushka sat by the window again and continued knitting a stocking.

Time was dragging on before Klimich's arrival. I walked around from room to room. I was either really hot or shivering. The sun broke into the room and disappeared behind the snowy clouds. The wind was howling. But then a gray veil of the sunset appeared behind the window. The bell rang. It was as if electricity had passed through me.

Shaking the snow off his coat, Klimich happily said: "Look how much white bread they gave me, it's enough for the road, and we will share it."

"Good evening! It's a good thing you came by," said my father, starting a conversation with Klimich. "When are you off to the front?"

"Well, my time is up today," replied Klimich.

"Where do you serve, if you don't mind me asking?" inquired my father.

My father invited Klimich to his office. All three of us went there. It was my father's favorite thing to show people his butterfly collection.

Klimich carefully examined all of my father's proud collection.

"Can I offer you a smoke?" Klimich offered my father cigarettes.

"I don't smoke those. I prefer a pipe or a cigar," my father replied.

Klimich looked at his box of cigarettes, twirled it around, and put it in his pocket. In a minute, he took it out again and opening it, pulled out a cigarette and lit it.

"Will you have some beer?" my father asked Klimich.

"With great enjoyment" Klimich replied, crossing his legs on the couch.

"How amazing; so you say that every single one of these things has its own name?" Klimich asked.

"Yes, every single one has its own passport," my father replied, and looking at our guest, my father moved a glass of beer to him.

"They killed Rasputin, sir. I think that soon enough the whole crew will be finished. What do you think about this?" Klimich asked.

Trying to avoid the topic, my father said: "You know, I'm not really interested in politics, I am more interested in science."

Shaking his head, Klimich blurted out: "What about your daughter, sir? To tell the truth, you are a nice fellow, reasonable, so what do you say?"

The cup of beer shook in my father's hand, the beer spilled on his beard. He was completely shocked. Slamming his fist on the table, he yelled: "Leave my Zina alone! She isn't going anywhere! I thought you were a good person, but you are a troublemaker! Why are you confusing my daughter? I won't let her go!"

"Don't get too upset. It's not that big of a deal. Zina will make her own decisions. She isn't young anymore; she knows what she is doing," Klimich replied.

My father's eyes stared at me tearing, and Klimich's were burning. I was silent.

"Decide, Zina, right now," demanded Klimich.

"Well, yes, I will think about it," I said.

Klimich nodded his head to my father and walked out.

I was sad to upset my father, but I firmly decided to go with Klimich. And what I was so certain of last night seemed so much harder now, to leave home and have to tell him that. I'm going to go, but I won't see my father's pain. I will do it behind his back. That seemed easier.

I caught Klimich as he was leaving. "Klimich, wait a minute, you have to understand, I feel bad for him," I said.

"You have one father, but there are millions of people, decide for yourself," Klimich said to me.

"Go, Klimich, but wait for me at the train station," I answered. The door opened and slammed shut.

I returned to my father's office. He sat on the couch, his head bent and eyes closed. I walked backward quietly, then passed Alekseevnushka, who was busy sewing. My mother and Valya hadn't returned from visiting friends. An hour passed, maybe more. My father calmed down and walked around proudly. He didn't talk to me, but he thought that I changed my mind about leaving the house. Everyone went to bed early.

Without taking my clothing bag, throwing the strap of Yeriga's bag over my shoulder, I dressed quickly. I pulled down my hat to the tip of my ears.

Through the whirl of the snowstorm, lights appeared like the eyes of a wolf by the Volga.

The December wind blew up the ends of my coat. My feet drowned in heaps of snow. The dim shining from the lights by the dam made the snow sparkle. A three-horse carriage ran past. It was the coachman of General Sandetsky and became barely a silhouette in the distance. I didn't walk, I ran. The train station became clearer and clearer. My run that seemed about one hundred versts was over.

The station—platform disorder—Klimich—the whistle of the train. The sadness of leaving and again the rhythmic chugging of the wheels.

CHAPTER 12

Zina returns to her unit, and several months go by facing the
Austrian trenches. Some of her friends are killed by enemy
artillery fire, and she meets another female volunteer soldier
in a neighboring regiment.

After walking through the noisy streets of Tarnopol by the train station, we went to the head transportation officer.[1] There we got information about the approximate location of the Twelfth Division. Passing by the Yan Sobesky Square, we caught up with the wagons.

There were wagons filled with hay on the way to Buchach.[2] We asked the soldier in charge of supplies for permission to ride on top of the hay to Monastorzyska.[3] I felt like I was freezing sitting next to the driver. I was turning into an icicle.

"I won't make it to the division headquarters," I complained to the soldier.

"I tell you, why don't you climb over here?" he said.

Moving a stack of hay, he pointed to the parting he made. Climbing in between, I started getting warmer. The soldier got up a little and covered the opening he made for me with a coat. It became a hole with a roof.

"What about now?" asked Klimich. "Does it still blow?"

"It's better. I am getting warmer," I squeaked from the cave.

I fell asleep. The soldier sang. He sang close by me, but his voice sounded so far away:

My hut is small in the valley
In it, Dynashka, that beauty,
Raises her son
The bright day has come
The dew is on the ground
Dynashka's eyes gaze out the window
There is a sad dust on the road
The father is buried
He will not answer . . .

His voice broke off. The carts stopped.

)))

"Look guys, Zina came back!" someone shouted. Trofim was greeting me, and Chereshenko and Zaporozhets followed. As I gulped a huge cup of soda, the bubbles went to my nose, and my eyes teared. A wave of emotion came over me from the last few days. I remembered my mother, my father, Valya, Alekseevnushka, and for some reason, my old dog Toby, and the terrible cold on the way here, and now this encounter.

"I came back again. I am back again," I barely managed to blurt out as tears streamed down my face. Yeriga walked up to me. I looked at his thin waist pulled by his belt. He moved closer to me.

"Zina, Zina, why are you crying? Did someone do anything to you? Tell me," he said.

Yeriga stroked my cheek, and I don't know why, but that made me cry even more.

)))

Every morning there was fog. Sometimes the sun would come out and then drown in the clouds again. At noon there was an abrupt noise from an Austrian battery that destroyed a First Company dugout. My heart sunk.

Klimich lived there. It's where Chereshenko amused everyone with his jokes. Yeriga pulled me by my coat, and we ran to where the explosion took place.

They were already digging up people. You could see Chereshenko's foot emerging. A big chunk of dirt fell on his chest. His head was in the mud. He groaned. Zaporozhets leaned over his friend.

"It's me, Paval. Do you recognize me? Paval, you will live, oh God, you will make it."

He tried to reassure his badly wounded friend, nervously playing with his mustache.

"Gritsko, is that you? Don't you hear them, Gritsko? How beautifully they sing."

Chereshenko was silent, and Zaporozhets didn't hear his voice anymore.

Ishmael Khabulin's face was swollen. There was blood under his skin. One eye was open, and he struggled to open the other. It was covered in dirt. He was whispering something. I leaned over him and could barely decipher his words, "Three battalions . . . three battalions . . ."

The nurse said his name loudly, "Ishmael!" Khabulin would not answer.

"He can't hear anything," said the nurse, as he put cotton in Khabulin's ears.

Klimich was dead. His opened mouth was stuffed with dirt. There was a piece of a shell sticking out from his cheek. His orange beard was soaked in blood. Trofim took Klimich's hands and crossed them on his chest. He covered the dead body with a rough tent. I couldn't bear to look at them any longer. I pulled Yeriga away from the wall of the dugout. They carried Klimich away on the stretchers right in front of us. Trofim and Zaporozhets followed the stretchers with their hats in their hands.

I walked around for a long time, passing one company then the next. I didn't even notice how I walked past my own regiment to the start of the Sebastopol Regiment's trenches. I slowed down, and then I quickened my pace. I couldn't get rid of the image in my mind of Chereshenko's huge foot.

Not too far away I saw a shovel. Walking past it, I touched it. It fell. A frozen piece of dirt followed it. I got scared from the sound of the falling shovel and quickly ran away, shaking. I ran into the Sebastopol Regiment's underground command post.

"Hello," the officers greeted me. "You came to visit? Well come on in then. Why are you so scared?" asked one of them, and he put a cup of tea on the stove.

I still couldn't come to terms with what had happened. Sitting down for a little, I calmed down a bit. They all drank tea here. They crunched on cubes of sugar and ate heavily salted black bread. I don't know why, but this scene calmed me. I got really hungry all of a sudden. I asked for a piece of bread from an officer. They cut up sausage and offered me some. I ate without chewing.

One of the officers sitting here looked familiar. I've seen him before. Underneath his cap, his blond hair flowed down to his shoulders. He furrowed his brow, and stretching out his neck, he looked into his neighbor's slanted eyes. His big, thin nose was slightly pointed. After drinking tea, he wiped the sweat from his head. The dirt that was on his face and neck came off on the handkerchief. Stretching out on the metal spring bed, he started singing, "Gaudeamus igitur."[4] I heard that tune from Valya's teacher Innokenty.

"Klimich and Chereshenko were killed," I said.

"Who are they?" an officer asked.

"People from our platoon," I replied.

"People! That is a pity. A pity," the officer said in a deep voice and threw a hostile glance at another officer.

"All right, well, I will go now," I said.

"Why are you staying such a short while?" asked an officer.

"I don't know, I am just walking around. It's boring around here. Klimich is gone. Chereshenko is gone."

I thought the officer would understand.

"We have somewhat of an example of you here too. I thought that you came to visit her," said an old officer in my direction.

"No, I stumbled upon you. Where is your volunteer?" I asked.

"Anisov!" yelled the officer.

"That's right, sir, I am Anisov."

A soldier appeared in the doorway, whose jacket had a burn mark through it. His eyes looked like grapes in dough. He had a really fat face. His big mouth was smiling.

"You can't go without saying your name can you, you prankster Anisov!"

"That's right, sir, prankster Anisov."

"All right take our guest to the artillery battery. She has a friend there. Got it?" said the officer.

"Anisov got it, sir, don't worry," he replied.

)))

There air was bad, and it was crowded in the artillery battery's housing.

Surrounded by soldiers, sitting on a pile of wood, was the volunteer of the Sebastopol Regiment. Seeing me, the big-breasted, wide-hipped woman got up and extended her wide hand to me.

"Sit down, you'll be our guest," the brunette said to me. Her eyes opened wider, and her gaze fell on my medal. Her big red lips were smiling.

"What did you get it for? For something real or just something small?" she asked me in a deep voice.

I didn't like her question, and I wanted to say something rude, but instead I said shyly: "I don't know."

"Why did you go to war?" the woman asked me again, as she bent down and picked up a cigarette butt from the floor and put the tobacco onto a piece of newspaper and started rolling it.

I decided not to be shy here and took out cigarettes from my pocket. I offered her one and lit one up myself, immediately coughing.

"Are you pulling on it? Well, pull, pull." And crossing her legs she asked me again: "Why did you go war?"

"I just went," I said.

"What does that mean? For no reason?" she asked. She cursed. The soldiers laughed. I just stood there.

"All right, Steshka, don't overdo it. Why are you starting with her? They say she has been in the trenches with the Stavropolsky crowd for a while now. Prove yourself first," said a soldier who defended me.

He boosted up my confidence, and once shy and confused by this lax woman, I asked: "Do you know how to shoot, Steshka?"

"No, but it's not a problem. I will learn. Don't be all polite with me," she answered, not intimidated by me in the least.

"Okay, then tell me why you went to war," I asked. I stared into her brown eyes.

"I came to war to seek revenge on the Germans for killing my love, my husband Ignat," she said, and she moved closer to a soldier.

No, I thought. That's not why you came. Don't even think that! I know exactly why you came!

I wanted to talk more with this woman, but the artillerymen were getting ready to go to sleep. Saying good-bye to my new acquaintance, I went back to my regiment.

I couldn't sleep. I lay on my cot, watched the fire and, for some reason, I remembered one of our marches. We were going to the reserve lines. On a rough winter day there was a soldier that walked in front of me. The soldier wore shoes made of straw. I remember one of them was ripped. His heel was sticking out, and it was red. I guess he didn't have *portjanki*. When we took a break, he took off his shoe and tried to warm his foot with his breath. When we took off again, he walked along saying: "Oh, my poor foot, my poor, poor foot." We went on for another verst, and again I saw his red heel. He walked on with some kind of completely stupid patience, and when we stopped at a village, there was a call for everyone to step up, and when that soldier didn't, the brigade commander, in his comfortable warm boots with fur inside, came up to the poor soldier and hit him. The soldier took out a handkerchief, put it to his bleeding ear, and with the same stupid patience, he walked back into the hut.

"What are you thinking about, Zina?" Trofim interrupted my train of thought, as he sat down next to me. I said: "For some reason I'm really sad, Trofim. Tell me about the Carpathian Mountains. Remember you promised?"

Trofim took off his boots, hung up his portjanki, and wrapped his feet in a scarf and explained:

"So this is what happened, Zina. We held Mezo Laborez, and then we left and went to take our new positions.[5] The Germans fired on us. The fire was accurate and intense. This is where the trouble was, Zina. You couldn't carry the wounded out of there. My neighbor was wounded. His legs were broken. 'Take me out of here, I'm going to freeze. I will die,' he pleaded. How could we carry him? There was a storm, and the road was nonexistent, being a downward slope covered with snow. The only way out was a small, snow-covered trail. We pulled him to the side and stopped. The slope was about five versts. It was pretty scary."

"Maybe you were on the wrong road? How did the field kitchens follow you?" I asked.

"What kitchens, Zina? We spent many days there without hot food. But I have to tell you, we got him down. But there was another problem. Now we had to carry him, and there was no other way to go. Nurse Kolka Filin and I struggled up there. We were sweating so much that we didn't even feel the cold. It was tough with him, but how could we leave him? It would not be in accordance with a Christian soul. It was so hard, what were we to do? When I remember that moment in my life, I don't even have the words to explain everything. Semenich was freezing, and he couldn't take it anymore. He did not even hold on to the stretcher. He bit into the cloth and said: 'Guys, leave me. I can't go on like this. But I have only one request, kill me. Shoot, Terekhin, I would rather die instantly then suffer this pain.' What was I to do now? But when we stopped, we started to freeze. The nurse said to me: 'He is starting to freeze, just leave him. It will be the same thing anyway.'"

"What did you do, Trofim? Did you shoot him?" I asked.

"No, Zina. He couldn't take the pain anymore. He rolled down the hill himself. We almost died. We began to climb uphill quickly. We heard an animal. The wolves were near Semenich. We should have opened fire on one of them to prevent him from nearing Semenich's body, but we were in such shock and so scared that we hurried up the hill even faster. It's such a sin, Zina. No prayers would help him. I will never forget the Carpathian Mountains! So many people died there, Zina! Sleep now!"

CHAPTER 13

In March 1917, revolutionary forces take hold after the czar's abdication. Unrest in the army increases.

In the morning there were rumors spreading through the trenches that the czar had been overthrown.[1] The officers tried to cover up this news; they constantly whispered about it and gathered in their dugouts. Trofim stood by the door of the dugout, and crossing his chest, he kept repeating: "Oh God, what's going to happen now? They overthrew the czar."

Yeriga, cleaning his boots, looked at Trofim and said: "What are you whining about? What happened we saw, but what is to happen, we shall see."

"Good day to you!" said Zaporozhets, standing in the doorway. He had a bag made of thick, waterproof fabric hanging over his shoulder. He dug through it, and when he found a letter, he pulled it out and handed it to me.

"Here! Take it! The commander gave it to me to pass on to you. I live like a boss now. It's good to be responsible for army communications, but I am hurting a little--Chereshenko isn't here," he said.

The letter was from Sasha. My heart beat exactly once, twice and practically stopped.

> Zinochka, I finally found you! Even though I have a lot of worries right now, I will be with you guys in a day or two. I am still

very loyal to you. I send you too many kisses to count. Your Alexander Petrovich Gusev, senior telephone operator at brigade headquarters.

The dugout was filled with many soldiers. After reading it a few times, I memorized it and put it away. The soldiers didn't stop talking for a minute. A lot of them thought that they would be starting on leave from the army tomorrow. They reminisced about their homes and their families. One soldier said: "I think, guys, that now our food will be better, since so much money was spent on the czar for his clothes, tasty food for him, for all his rides, and his nights out."

"According to my understanding, they will be declaring peace soon because Russia's gotten poor, and nothing good has happened until now. Whoever is going to be in power next will want to show how good they are now. They will call us back, I tell you!" another soldier declared.

They talked a lot and for a long time. It seemed as if tomorrow or the next day, or really, really soon, they would get to see their wives and children.

))}

The days passed. There was no one released from the army. The food didn't get any better. Soldiers continued to get killed. The wounded groaned as usual, and soldiers fell to the ground at every bullet that was fired.

Huddling together after their work was done, they discussed the news brought from the rear of the army:

"You say there is a revolution? A revolution, that's what David Markovitch spoke of. Now, guys, the people will have a voice. Now everything is ours. The revolution, brother, now means that we will have peace. And now they will ask us if we want to fight, we will, and if we don't want to fight, we won't. They have to ask the people everything. Do you understand what kind of a revolution this is?"

"Whether we are fighting or not, we don't know, but we were told not to put down our arms and stay by our swords," explained a soldier.

"We have to do away with this war. We will not go against the Germans. We will not go against our working brothers. You understand?" argued another.

"To hell with these arms. What do we need them for? Away with them until next time," added another.

"You defended someone else's belongings, but you will not defend your own?" someone asked.

"What do we need arms for? Throw down your swords! We don't want to fight anymore!" shouted someone else.

"Guys, do what he says here, we don't know too much here. We have to listen to those who know what is going on," cautioned another.

"Say 'Tovarisch,' not 'my brother'!² This is the way it should be," echoed a final comment.

))⟩

The snow was melting. It was foggy in the morning. The dampness sank through the skin. We dried our coats by the fire. The boot leather was warping out of shape and drying up; it shriveled. We could barely put on our boots. The water poured through all the holes and cracks in the dugout.

At night, when the guards switched, soldiers warmed up tea. Reaching for his cup, Yeriga, seeing a big toad on his cot, jumped from the surprise.

"You bitch, you think you're getting comfortable here!" he said. He took off his belt, and raising his hand to hit it, apparently changed his mind and tried to push the toad away with his spoon. The ugly, brown-spotted thing didn't move.

"So, you are going to sit there?" asked Yeriga. "The wetness makes you happy, but for me, my bones are aching. Fine, sit there, we have enough space."

"Trofim, what are you thinking about?" Yeriga asked.

"Everything is so boring. I sit on the ground, but I miss my land. I wish we could go home. It will be time to cultivate the soil soon. But here we're not getting anything done. Grief takes hold of you. Maybe we won't even make it to the end. After all, Klimich died. I'm sick of it here, I'm sick of it," Trofim complained.

Heavy drops of water fell from the ceiling, hitting the hot stove. The toad croaked.

"So what, big deal, the czar is gone," Trofim said, sitting down next to Yeriga.

"And now what? Nothing! Everything is the way it was before. The positions are so horrible today, the roads are so slippery and muddy, and we're not getting any warm food tonight. I actually saw Captain Krapivansky today, and he said, 'Comrades, a little longer and the war will be over.'"

⟩⟩⟩

The snow was melting, and you could see the ground. There were birds all over above the trenches. The sharp March wind tickled my face. It was impossible to walk through the trenches. There was water up to your knees.

I had been working as a nurse for many days now. I wrote a letter home:

> Don't worry. I'm healthy. I send kisses to everyone. Valya! Send a package. I can't write anymore, I don't have time. There is a lot of work to be done.
>
> *Zina*

"Zina, get to the Fourth Division, they're calling you!" Yeriga yelled to me. He was sewing his coat, shortening it up to his waist.

"Yeriga, why do you wear such a short coat?" I asked, interested.

"What do you mean why? Because that's my style! Go, Zina, they're calling you. You heard?"

Zaporozhets walked toward me in water up to his waist before I got to the Eighth Company. Krivdin was on his back with his feet dangling. Krivdin yelled at Zaporozhets: "Bend over, you son of a bitch! Carry me a little further."

Zaporozhets walked through the water with his head bent. Krivdin sat on his shoulders. Krapivansky walked up behind Zaporozhets and pulled on his coat. The bravery of the captain surprised everyone. Zaporozhets tripped, and Krivdin fell in the water. He wallowed for a while in the puddle. People surrounded him, but nobody helped him get up.

"I'll show you, I will arrest you all," threatened Krivdin.

"Who are you going to fight with?" said a voice from the dark. "You rode on a soldier's back, enough."

Captain Krapivansky joked the whole way, but Krivdin scrambled, tripping from one pothole to the next.

)))

The left and right flank of the Stavropolsky Regiment trenches were located on higher ground, and from there all the snow was melting. The water poured endlessly right to the middle of their section. In certain places the dugouts were flooded. We moved from one dugout to the next, trying to save ourselves from the water. There were so many people in our dugout, you could barely move.

"Thank God, the Kybansky Regiment is coming to replace us!" Yeriga brought this good news when he came back from the village. There was one day left until they were to arrive. The water poured mercilessly.

"Trofim, let's go, Captain Krapivansky ordered us to gather by the First Company," Yeriga urged.

I needed to get medicine and a bandage from Nayumich, so I followed them.

We had a whole day left before the replacements arrived. The soldiers were building a dam under the command of Captain Krapivansky. They carried bags of dirt and shovels. At the juncture where the First and Second Battalion met, they threw down their loads. Everyone worked with their shovels digging, throwing dirt in the walkways. The same thing was done by the Fourth Company. By the evening our dam was ready. The soldiers successfully got all the water out of the trenches in a few hours, without a break. It now became easier to walk through the trenches.

All of our stuff was ready, and so we were to head out by the eve of the next day. We were just leaving the dugouts when all the water we worked so hard to hold back came crashing down. It went directly through the communications trench and flooded all of the trenches. Krapivansky's voice came from somewhere: "Asses, what asses! They shot right through our wall!"

When we were walking up to our stomachs in water, some soldier's boots fell off. He got on top of the dam we had made and sat there with a pathetic look on his face. In about two minutes, he was wounded. No one paid any attention to him, everyone just thought about how they could get out of there quicker.

It was completely dark by the time we all got out of the dugouts and walked through the valley. But it wasn't any easier. The mud sucked our feet in. It was some kind of wild march of the regiment. As if on command, one soldier would bend down, pull his boot out of the dirt, then the next and the next. The night was dark, and people walked bumping into each other, cursing absolutely everything. And the enemy fired shrapnel after shrapnel, getting nice, clean, and easily reachable shots at us.

"Damn them. We allowed them to take the higher ground, and we stayed in the valley. Idiots, brainless," cursed Krapivansky loudly, without any shame.

"We should have climbed higher. It would have been easier for both sides," a voice said.

)))

The regiment was at rest. The sun enveloped the fields, and there were some distant tunes of birds in the forest on this spring day. What a strange day! No fire at all. Our soldiers walked around.

"Friends, the Austrians are fraternizing with our men in the Twelfth Division. Hurray friends!" shouted Trofim. "Hurray! Hurray! They are fraternizing!" he repeated.

Yeriga threw up his hat, and Trofim crossed his chest. I looked at Yeriga. I was cheerful, and the day was as bright as ever.

"Comrade Zina!" called Ivanov. I turned around. At that moment I felt like the sun got brighter, and the sky got bluer, and the spring day was a pleasant tune.

"Comrade Zina!" Ivanov called again. That was the first time he had ever called me comrade. At first I answered him just as simply as he would answer me.

"Let's make friends with the Austrians tomorrow," I suggested.

"And me too," jumped up Yeriga, tightly pulling in his belt.

"In the spring everything is mellow," Trofim smiled.

"What about you, Trofim? How are you?" asked Yeriga.

"I am all right, but it's about time to plow the fields," Trofim replied.

)))

In the hut our regimental commander's orderly complained to us:

"I bring him more and more iodine. He drinks it and drinks it 'For my body's health.' Yesterday he summoned Dybelo to deliver packages for Galinka, the landlady's daughter. Every day he takes bags and bags there. I heard it myself when he said to her that he is treating her to everything, and it all came with regards from Colonel Plakhov. He told her she should sleep with the colonel one night, and he would give her lots of presents. She told him to leave her alone and go away. As Dybelo was leaving her house, her lover Kolka Ushatin was coming."

"You should have told Captain Krapivansky that he is trying to steal the soldier's girl," someone commented.

"I told him, I told him everything," said the orderly.

Everyone shut up. There was a loud scream from outside.

"I'll order you to be beaten! Don't touch her. Don't touch her, I tell you! Let her go, you son of a bitch!" shouted Captain Krapivansky.

We ran out onto the porch. Dybelo was dragging Galinka by the hand, and she was struggling against him, crying and scratching Dybelo's arms.

Captain Krapivansky was yelling: "Let her go, I say!"

The girl fell down on her knees. Dybelo wouldn't let her go. The soldiers gathered, watching the captain and waiting for a command. Plakhov's servant ran up to the captain and said: "Sir, the regimental commander would like to see you."

"All right, here we go, it has started," said Krapivansky's servant.

"Zina, as soon as it gets dark, go with Yeriga and see what is happening over there, okay? We're all curious. All right?" asked a soldier.

"I will, I will," I said, and I followed the servant.

Yeriga and I got near Plakhov's window. It got dark. I stood by the regimental commander's window and watched with one eye. I had to slant my eye, as I couldn't see well. I didn't get the opportunity to go right up to the window and watch. While I was getting settled in, they were already speaking about something. I heard Plakhov's words: "You are a young captain, and a good one, but how dare you threaten my policeman? How dare you?"

I saw the regimental commander nearing the captain, and the captain moved backward and picked up his sword. Plakhov got nearer again and yelled: "You are a young captain! You don't have the right to!"

Krapivansky slightly pulled out his sword. The colonel immediately started walking backward. The captain said: "What is the problem, Colonel? What is the problem? Please explain it to me."

Plakhov was really red, and backing away, he shook his beard, leaning on a table and said: "Answer me, Captain, what right did you have? How dare you?"

The captain spoke to the colonel again: "Mr. Colonel, what's the problem? I don't understand what the problem is? I threatened a military policeman. What do you say about that?"

"I will arrest you, Captain! How dare you!" yelled Plakhov, avoiding the captain's question. He added: "I command you to shut up. Get out."

I moved away from the window to take a breath. The door slammed. The captain walked out. We ran over by the stairs. Krapivansky was walking down the steps. The handless Melnikov walked towards him.

"Sergey! He didn't have the guts to admit his terrible behavior! He didn't even say a word about how he steals women! He should be ashamed!" said Krapivansky.

"All right, Nicolai, all right! So he annoyed you, you say?" laughed Melnikov, and taking the captain under the arm, turned into the street.

That evening the soldiers gathered by the church and danced to the music of Yeriga's balalaika. Galinka came out pretentiously into the middle of the circle. Kolka followed her, stamping his feet sideways. Galinka spun around, hitting her boyfriend with her long braid.

The next day we found out about Krapivansky's arrest, and the whole regiment knew the situation with Galinka.

)))

It's quiet on the front lines. Soldiers on both sides weren't shooting. Several soldiers walked on top of the traverse. The Austrians were visiting the Fourth Company. One of them treated Trofim to some rum. Trofim took a gulp and smiling, he wiped his beard and commented: "It's good, nice and sweet. Thank you."

Yeriga stretched his hand out, reaching for a cigar. An Austrian bit of the end of the cigar and handed it to him. He inhaled it and started coughing, saying: "It's strong; hell, it's really strong."

The Austrians laughed, but they weren't laughing at Yeriga, it was a genuine laugh. They pointed at his tiny waist, making a big circle with their forefingers and thumbs, saying: "Wie ein Weinglaschen!"[3]

A fat Austrian took out a newspaper and gave it to Yeriga. It said in Russian: "Soldiers read all." It said for all soldiers to throw down their arms and head home. Yeriga took the newspaper and put it under his cap. The Austrians treated me to some chocolate. They didn't stop staring at me. I really liked a tall, handsome Austrian. I didn't want them to leave. I offered him a big piece of bread. He didn't take it from me, but somehow ripped it away. He looked at it for a long time, then hiding it in his bag, he took my hand, kissed the palm of it, and taking out his picture, he put it there. Then he kissed my hand again.

Our guests left, and I looked at them for a long time. A shell that blew up near them made me run for cover. Then Lieutenant Colonel Krivdin's cursing was heard: "What a disgrace! A disgrace! What the hell is this? Fraternizing? Separate! Take your places! Separate immediately! Separate, you sons of bitches!"

Nobody listened to him. Austrians appeared all over the trenches.

)))

We had Austrian visitors very often. But I really wanted to go visit them. And finally I got my chance too. It was a warm spring day. Yeriga and I walked in the direction of the Austrian trenches, to the left of us another group of soldiers did the same.

There were three Austrians sitting down, and a fourth, an old German, was bent over a real enamel sink washing his face with soap. He wiped his face with a towel and then sprayed himself with real cologne. Turning around, his gaze fell on me. How could I explain to him that my friend and I came to visit them? A fat German twisting his mustache sat down next to me. It was very hard to explain things to him.

They prepared cocoa. There was no bread. We chewed on cookies. For a second, silence set in. Then the German got up off a bed covered in a brown blanket and ran to his book bag, took out a camera wrapped in velvet and asked me to come outside. Yeriga looked at me with questioning eyes and tried to hide his upset face. I pulled him by the arm, and the three of us went out into an underground trench tunnel that was really wide and tall. There the German showed us where to stand, and Yeriga, next to me, straightened his back, pulled down his coat, and straightened his arms by his sides. The German smiled. I stood next to him. He took a picture. Then I posed again, batting my eyes.

The fire had begun so suddenly. Shells were exploding. Lost, Yeriga and I looked at each other, but we weren't scared. I looked at him, and he looked at me, and we both burst into laughter.

"Zina, what do we do now? If there were to be an attack, what would we do? Maybe the war is really over? Let's go, Zina! What if we get stuck here? How will I get home to my village?" he started saying with a hint of worry in his tone.

The Austrians showed us a covering where we could sit it out. And the fat German said: "It will all be over soon."

We had to sit there with the Austrians through the fire, then walking through their dugouts, I looked at all the people, but unfortunately the one I was looking for wasn't there. The fat one, noticing that I was looking for someone, said: "Suchen Sie Jemanden?"[4]

"Yes," I answered and took out the picture that was given to me to show him.

"Oh! Kohgler! Er ging nach ihre Richtung, war verwundet und ewakuirt."[5]

Why did that happen though? Why didn't I get his address? Maybe he thought of it himself and wanted to come give it to me? I will probably never see him again now!

A shrapnel shell exploded above the trenches. Yeriga and I hurried up, running back to our trenches.

)))

The Stavropolsky Regiment took up their positions in the town of Stanislau after a long march.[6] The bright spring sun and light wind dried up the ground. Nature turned green again. There were a lot of tables in a big yard. There were ten benches brought from the school. They covered the tables with tablecloths, and dishes were brought out from the priest's house. Wines and liquors adorned the table. Colonel Plakhov, leaning on his big familiar wooden stick, invited the officers to the table. The officers indulged in the food and crunched loudly on pig skins. Glasses were filled, speeches were given, and toasts were made. They drank to the health of the ministers of the Provisional Government. They yelled "hooray" for Minister of War Kerensky and "hooray for the brave commanders of the Russian army!"[7] They drank to the health of Colonel Plakhov too.

On a stool at the corner of the table sat soldier Derevanchenko, temporary head of the regimental committee.[8]

"Derevanchenko would like to say a few words" said Plakhov in a nasal voice, and not holding back his anger very well, sat down in his seat, shoving his stick into the ground.

Derevanchenko got up and asked: "I have one question for the officers. Everyone said their speeches. We all heard them. But why didn't anyone toast to the regimental committee?"

He wiped the sweat from his forehead and sat back down. No one answered him. Everyone was quiet. After a minute, Lieutenant Colonel Krivdin offered a toast to "protecting our freedom and fighting the war until its victorious end."

Filling up my bag with medicine, I walked outside in the direction of the trenches. I forgot a bottle of iodine, and walking all the way back, I searched for it. It got dark, and I decided just to sleep here.

There was a dim light in the room. There was wallpaper on the walls. There were many postcards on the walls, out of which lice peeked out. A picture of a woman in a shell-decorated frame stood on a chest of drawers. I looked at the cat-eyed beauty in the picture.

Outside the artillery moved loudly along the rocky road. For a few days, from morning until night, heavy and light batteries were on the move. Huge amounts of ammunition were brought in. There was a large number of artillery pieces brought toward Stanislau. Everyone spoke about a big attack. People said that never in their lives had they seen this much artillery throughout the whole war. Today I saw a Cossack regiment of the "Savage Division" on Sapezhinsky Street.[9] Coming from the division headquarters, a messenger brought news that they are waiting for the Minister of War Kerensky to arrive any day. They said he makes great speeches and will address the people in Stanislau. I was curious to see him. After all, I had heard so much about him. I was even considering staying a day or two in the town.

A scream; a girl ran into the room. Her black hair was a mess. The homeowner's daughter, returning from a dark corner of the city, ran into an officer of the Savage Division. She told how he grabbed her by the fence and raped her. The beauty was shaking from crying. Her mother slouched against the wall by an open door, banging on it. She cried too. An old voice said a prayer from the next room. The clock was ticking, and on the roof cats meowed loudly.

)))

At noon, lining up in formation, the soldiers tensely awaited the arrival of the Minister of War. The noise of a motor was heard. The car stopped on Sapezhinsky Street. "Hoorays!" were heard throughout the town.

Kerensky, with one hand behind his back and leaning on the podium, began to speak. He spoke for a long time. He tried to convince the soldiers that they had to fight this war until its victorious end. He spoke about defending freedom. He called the soldiers eagles and said they had spirit. He kept saying that the Provisional Government was confident in the victory of Russian soldiers, and that the next attack would be the last and a victorious one, adding, "and with this victory we will be closer to the peace."

Most of the soldiers listened to Kerensky with their mouths hanging open; some cried. I saw the face of a soldier who was unable to stop drool from coming out of his mouth, and when Kerensky ended his speech by saying, "we are with you and we will not leave you," that soldier pushed his way to the front and fell at Kerensky's feet. I sat on the fence, and I could see how his brown boots glistened in the sun. I saw how the skinny soldier with three St. George crosses covered Kerensky's boots with kisses as he yelled: "Is it really true that you are with us? Is this really the last attack? Is it really true there will be peace?"

After Kerensky's speech General Brusilov spoke.[10] The face of the general was very pale, with a big, deep wrinkle on his forehead. The start of his speech was met with hurrahs. The general didn't speak for long, he just said that it would be hard and painful for him to lose faith in the strength of the mighty Russian army. The soldiers cheered loudly after his last words. Melnikov stood next to me and whispered to Captain Krapivansky: "Look, Albert Thomas is going to speak. We will listen to the Frenchman."[11]

But Melnikov was wrong. Nobody else spoke. The Minister of War's car drove away, creating a cloud of dust. The soldiers stood there and watched the car. They had strange expressions on their faces, as if they were waiting for more. One of the soldiers asked another: "Why didn't the minister tell us anything about the factories? Or why didn't he tell us about the workers delegation? We demand an explanation!"

)))

Captain Krapivansky, standing on a stool surrounded by soldiers, was speaking: "I told you already that our mission is to check on the actions of the commanders. And we have to demand that the government ends the war quickly. I am done speaking. Hooray to peace, no more war! Hooray!"

"Hooray!" hundreds of soldiers yelled.

Stavropolsky Regiment soldiers listened intently the whole time. When he got off the stool, they swarmed around him and started asking questions, interrupting each other: "They will let us go? How many people will go to St. Petersburg as delegates? Maybe it's better to send Vaska Koravin? Maybe the officers should go?"

The captain barely got away, and he was on his way to the school. Melnikov walked up to him and said: "You see, Sergey, the soldiers responded to the regimental committees. Now we trust the picture is clear for them. If Zambor were to come back right now, these guys would kill him in a second!"

Above the city, either flying high or coming down low was a German airplane. Somewhere in the distance gunfire was heard. High above the airplane shrapnel exploded—gunfire; now lower. The gray "bird" fluttered its wing and went in the direction of May Third Street. Again a bomb exploded, and the battery's fire followed it.

I stood on the balcony of a two-story house where the division hospital was. Right next to me stood a Georgian nurse staring through her binoculars. She was impressed by the antiaircraft battery's precise shooting.

"Look, they're so precise! Take him down!" she urged.

There was a quick motion of an explosion, and there was a ball of fire in the air.

"What are you standing there for? Let's go and see!" the nurse urged.

The gracious Georgian girl, holding up her long skirt, quickly ran down the stairs. I saw her white headscarf run right past me from the balcony.

I stood on the balcony for a while. The ball of fire I just saw now was a bloody mass, and the once-blue sky seemed tainted red to me.

)))

It was the evening. There was no commotion, just silence.

They stood by the wire fence. The young boy was nineteen, and the rosy-cheeked girl was sixteen. The sunset was a like magical fairy dust above their heads.

I walked past carefully, my feet barely touching the ground. I was dizzy with the smell of spring. There, in the garden by the cherries, Sasha waited for me.

"Hi! I came."

"Zina, my sweet!"

Sasha hugged me tightly. We kissed passionately. A bat spreading its wings flew past in the evening hours. The ground was covered in dew. Somewhere in the distance, frogs croaked.

The garden was lit up. The night was gone. There was a loud singing coming from outside, a revolutionary march.

Sasha picked up his hat from the ground and a newspaper titled *The Truth about the Trenches* fell out.[12] We left the garden.

)))

Night; sometimes the shutters clacked. There were searchlights scanning the front lines. There was quiet talk in the trenches. You couldn't hear the ringing of the telephone in the communications trench. The officers didn't walk by. Three soldiers sat on a stack of hay. The fourth was getting up from the ground and said: "All right then, fellows, so we have to tell the leaders to end this war, and that's it. No more talking! Got it? That's all we have to say."

Sasha was in the doorway. He fixed his coat, hanging from his shoulders, on which he had a huge red bow and said: "Comrades, we will still have to fight. It's for our land and our interests. Nobody throw down their arms, but take them home with you. We need to send messages, one after the other, to end the war. Comrades, this is not our revolution, we have to break the generals first then the priests."

Taking a break, he lifted up the tent by its opening and listened. He added: "The Provisional Government is lying to us. We have to end this and establish our own regime. Our government will end the war and stand for peace. Our land has to belong to the peasants. We have a new front now—against the capitalists. I am done, my friends, I will not shout hurrah because we are in the trenches."

"That's right! That's right!" the soldiers responded.

"You speak the truth! We understand! Speak more!" they shouted.

"Now I will have a word!" announced Yeriga, jumping out into the middle.

"Speak! Speak!" they shouted.

"Comrades! I ask for your attention! We have to let the leaders know about Colonel Plakhov. We took enough of his shit! Enough! We should make them cut off his hands because his fists are merciless. Tell Captain Krapivansky, hurry! I am done!"

The voices didn't stop until dawn.

)))

The rain was pouring down. The march was very tough. I was soaked and tired.

My landlady prayed all evening. She gets up only to fix the lamp and then she is back to praying. Her son is dying. An old healer woman came to visit her. She sat down on the bench and began to calm the woman down.

"No, nothing will help him, he has such a sickness, such a sickness," the old woman lamented.

The healer untied her scarf, took out dried plants, rubbed them in her hands, and put it under his shirt. Then she took some more, and after chewing it, she spit it out onto the huge inflammation on the boy's neck. Then both whispered something and went outside.

The raindrops hit the window. The light from the lamp hit the ceiling. The shadow was becoming smaller and smaller. The sick boy's snoring wasn't letting me sleep. The old woman listened to his snoring, and if it quieted down then she would turn and look at him.

I was starting to doze off, but I couldn't fall asleep. The snoring went on. I couldn't go out into the barn, it's damaged, and it was pouring outside. The old woman whispered something; the boy moaned. Tomorrow we were going to march again. I wanted to sleep. The sick boy was irritating me.

"I want to sleep! Let me sleep! Shut up!" I said it, and all of a sudden I was afraid of my own words. What was I saying? The old woman, listening to the snoring of her son, had hopes of his recovery. He was silent, tears fell down her face, her hands shook, and playing with the lace of her black scarf, she was tense. He groaned, and the mother got hope again. And me? I wanted it to be quiet. I was afraid, and then I began to pity myself. Somewhere from inside of me a voice said, you stopped being human, you animal! Grabbing my pillow, I dug my head into it, and I saw myself as a little girl, but again the voice said, that's not you, it's not you anymore, you are an animal! I bit the pillow in despair. I really had lost something childish, something real, something good, and it was something that I could never get back.

CHAPTER 14

In June 1917 Zina runs away in the middle of a violent enemy attack and has a breakdown. She becomes involved in the spread of revolutionary activism while recuperating in the hospital.

The day of the assault came. It was June 18. There was nonstop noise for the past few days. Our artillery fired repeatedly. With sunrise we opened artillery fire on the enemy's trenches. All the cracking, snapping, and popping blended into one continuous noise. You couldn't hear anything. In the chaos of all the noise, a human voice was so muffled; it was as if it came from deep inside the ground. To the right of us stood two trees, and it was strange to see them untouched. Shells were exploding on the enemy lines around them, tearing soldiers to pieces. Another explosion and the trees were still standing.

There was a roar of artillery—explosions. The village of Yamnytsya went up in flames on the right of the front lines.[1] There was a thick cloud of smoke in the sky, and all of a sudden, for exactly one moment, everything stood still as if they all agreed on it, and then there was one explosion, just one, and it seemed as if everything froze.

They ran with contorted faces; everyone ran, nobody stopped. Others ran towards them, their faces unseen. They moved closer, petrified of death, one dark mask. There was a hit—splashes of blood and then tortured screams of the people; grinding of teeth and muffled cries.

I saw Bashmakin. His head was hitting the ground. His body thrashed about in convulsions and was giving out. His was losing consciousness. He hit his head for the last time. He had no more strength left. He was helpless. His body twitched a few more times. His eyes froze with terror, and with blood gushing out of his mouth, he blurted his last words: "Take in the peace."

I had water in my canteen, one, maybe two gulps. I made a move to go to walk toward him when the ground underneath me shook. There was a loud noise over my head, I saw pieces of shrapnel around me, and as I covered my ears, I fell down onto the ground. I lay there on my side, and with my left hand I gave him water. Again his head beat against the ground. I couldn't watch his suffering any longer. I cried loudly and pulled him toward me. He pulled away, writhing in terrible agony. Looking up, I saw that person that just a second ago was alive, in contortions. He was dead. His last words had a scary, gruesome irony about them.

Someone ran past flailing his arms and fell to the ground. The shells started falling farther and farther away from us. A group of Austrians appeared unarmed, and they began moving in our direction. There was more, they were all running as they threw down their arms. There were shrapnel shells exploding above them in blue fireballs. That was the Austrian batteries firing at their own troops who were surrendering. The artillery fire was soon back in our direction.

)))

"Nu-u-r-se," a wounded soldier yelled. He sat there with his legs wide open, big drops of blood falling on his knees, then was rolling down on the ground. I jumped up, and throwing down my medicine pouch, I ran. I couldn't stay here any longer. I ran as if there were no one in my way. Someone yelled for me, but I ignored it and kept running. I was tripping over the dead and stepping on the wounded. I stepped on someone's arm and heard curses in my direction. I ran even faster. It was probably shameful, shameful to run from the place where people were dying, asking for my help. A few steps away a shell killed a soldier, and I reacted, I ran again, not answering to my conscience. I got to the reserve trenches. And here too, I found disheveled bodies. Someone grabbed my arm, and I ripped it away and kept up my embarrassing escape.

Running out onto the road, I was conscious of the sound of armored cars. They were headed in our direction from the Krimsky Regiment's position. Soldiers stood on the backs of them as they passed. A vanguard stood with banners on the cars. They had gold and silver chevrons with a skull and crossbones sewn on their arms.[2] A group of our retreating soldiers was headed right toward them. An officer, standing on the running board of the armored car, waved his sword. Machine guns fired; the soldiers throwing up their arms fell to the ground.

"They are shooting their own," a wounded soldier said, trying to get up.

I helped him; I wanted to help him see everything.

"It's the officers! Here let me help you up, you will see for yourself. All right, lie down now. See the bandage helped. Now you feel better," I said.

"Better; maybe I will make it home. I saw the Zaamyrtsev Regiment. They didn't go against the Austrians. Maybe the officers will kill the Zaamyrtsev troops," he said.

"You be quiet. Don't speak now. Calm down. You will feel better," I told him.

After seeing what happened, I left and ran towards the village. Here in the village of Pidpechery, a woman moaned about her dead calf.[3] I sat on a bench for a long time. Now the fire I heard was in the distance. I didn't know where I was going or who I was going to see. I moved my legs around aimlessly. I walked past a hut, there was a fire burning, I saw people, then they disappeared and reappeared again. There are probably wounded people on the floor. The doctors and nurses barely had time to apply bandages. I turned to the back of the house. People in white coats walked out. They carried a bucket covered in white cloth, and there was something in it. They went to the side of the garden and came back again. One of them was swinging the bucket that was now empty.

I sat down by the fence. The wind was gently blowing on my face. I wanted to sleep. I really wanted to sleep, my eyelids were closing. Forget . . . Screams . . . I jumped, startled. I got up and walked away to the other side of the garden. My hands felt extremely heavy. It was hard to keep my head in place. It felt like it was going to fall off. My legs wouldn't obey. They moved very slowly. A dog growled. Why was it growling? Was it protecting the garden? The dog kept growling. It could bite me! Let it bite me then, I thought. No, it won't bite me if I keep walking. I just have to walk with confidence, not the way I am. I started walking quickly, forcing my muscles to move. The dog continued to growl, and I thought I should take some dirt and throw it at the animal. But I was too lazy to bend down. I stretched my hand out and brushed my palm on poison ivy. I moved the bush with my foot and squeezed past sideways. Another dog had someone's amputated arm between its paws and was ripping the meat off of it. I walked on, and not too far away sat a white puppy. As the dog turned the hand in its paws, and the white puppy moved towards it, he growled. The moonlight fell on the bloody human bone. One move forward, and I felt like I was sinking. Then there was a scream, maybe it was my voice. I don't know, all I know is that right after that there were hundreds of other human voices yelling.

)))

The wide-open, bright rooms in which our hospital had settled was quickly filling up with people. Next to my cot lay what was left of Yeriga. It was like his shadow. He turned his thin body to me. His eyes looked like they fell into his face. He said:

"Well, how are you doing there? What happened to you? My sickness is light, but you, you're in deep. And every night you scream and moan. What made you come here if this is how you are? We all go because the government makes us, but you, no one forces you to do anything. You are insane!"

"Yeriga, why am I insane? You went, and I went."

"You are insane, and that's that. You chose your path with your own free will. Find another like you."

"There are other women fighting. You know Stesha? She's with the Sevastopolsky Regiment," I answered.

"Stesha? Oh, Zina! Stesha was a useful female for us soldiers. Not only did the Sevastopolsky soldiers know her, but so did we. She was fitting, but you? Someone touches you with a finger, and you're already down. But Stesha was . . ."

"You say was, but where is she now?" I asked.

"The Germans killed her. The Germans were counterattacking, and our troops began backing away, but she just continued forward, so they killed her. She got six bayonet wounds," he said.

"She went into battle?" I asked.

"She had a disease. What else was she to do with herself? Go home? She said it herself, she was spoiled here. She said she didn't want to work, so she decided her fate here," he explained.

"They stabbed her to death?" I asked.

"She was finished. Just wait, they will finish you off too. One time they'll miss you, the second time they'll miss you, but the third time they'll get you. You'll see," he said.

Yeriga called for a nurse and started fidgeting on his cot, holding his stomach.

))）

Our hospital section was one of the largest. Through the open doors you could see the corridors, and there to the right and left, there were more cots. The Austrians used to have a division hospital here. They left us foldable beds, stools, and boxes that held plates and utensils. Only the really sick used them. The soldiers were tired of washing up in the same old way, gargling water in their mouths, then spitting it out and washing their faces. Now, they filled up tubs with hot water and passed it around to wash off the dirt. A few times the nurses reminded the soldiers that they had sinks. The really weak didn't listen to the advice and continued to do what they were used to.

We got a lot of people who had typhus and dysentery. There was no room for them, so they had to be put in the section with the soldiers that hadn't yet been evacuated.

Lately the food wasn't fresh, and the tea smelled bad. The nurses told us that toads had died in the buckets and that was why the tea smelled so bad.

"Don't worry, guys, soon we will move, get some good food and head home," a wounded soldier said.

"You can't go there, you will fall. And you can't have any coffee either because you run around like the wind already," Yeriga commented, adding his thoughts.

"You can have the coffee when your stomach relaxes, as the doctor explained," the nurse said with authority.

)))

I lay in my bed, and I could see the starlit sky through the window. A meteor flew by. A small cloud covered the moon. It became dark in the room. My temperature rose again. My lips were dry, and I had an unpleasant taste of metal and bean soup in my mouth.

We heard explosions, even from here. It seemed as if they were close by. I saw the road clearly before me that led to the end of the village of Maidan.[4] Six explosions in one direction and then silence again. At sunrise there were nurses by me. They were lifting a soldier's body. His blue face had red blotches on it. He died at night from peritonitis. He lay there dead next to us, and only in the morning did we discover that he had died. There were orders given for a grave to be dug. All that was heard was the sound of shovels, and then they turned around and slowly walked away.

)))

The Austrians were firing artillery for three days straight. It seemed strange that the artillery of both sides was firing on just one area. Ours was moving forward, and I saw the officers of the Savage Division ride passed my window.

At night two soldiers of the Drozdovskoy Division walked in and started yelling at the nurse on duty, asking him for cocaine. A few more days passed, and we saw the Drozdovskoy Division's cavalry. One time Yeriga was so appalled by the yelling of one of the drunken cavalrymen that he threw his canteen at him. The guy threw down his coat and ran into the hospital. All the sick that could get up did, and there was a scuffle. All the doctors ran up. One of the really sick soldiers got hit in the stomach by the cavalryman. He fell on the floor holding his stomach. The soldiers beat the cavalryman with everything that was near them. Dr. DeMorrey put an end to everything, and they arrested the cavalryman and took him away. Now every night a watchman stood by the doors.

)))

Krivdin was getting his arm bandaged. His index finger was bitten off by a German officer. He told the nurses about the night attack, when he bumped into the German in the trenches. The German, trying to get the pistol out of his hand, bit off half his finger.

"And you know what else doctor, there were soldiers from my own battalion nearby, and none of them offered me help. Doctor, tell me why does it hurt so badly? I was wounded twice before, but this pain is the worst I've felt," complained Krivdin.

"I am going to have to disappoint you, Colonel, I think the German had bad teeth. You might have an infection," the doctor cautioned.

Krivdin's face turned into an ugly grimace. He was helped into a bed, and the doctor followed with a thermometer. The next morning a nurse told us he died.

)))

The regiment moved five more versts, and they didn't have time to evacuate everyone, so some people were moved to the village of Vistova.[5] I was getting better, and lying in confinement was getting annoying to me. You wake up in the morning and see Vaska's sleepy face. Then all the tying of the bandages, the applying of the medicine, and the checking of the temperature begins. None of the sick were interested in the movements or actions of the regiment; everyone just wanted to leave quickly.

If someone was brought in that had an unusual disease or wound, everyone would get up from their cots to watch the soldier's suffering. Each one of them suffered in their own way. One of them would just clench his teeth and suffer silently, and another would yell for a nurse, a doctor, and when they would come, he would grab their hand

and moan, "oh, doctor, oh, doctor!" or "oh, mommy, oh, mommy!" Sometimes we would discuss it before they carried a soldier out. Yeriga would ask: "Will he be a loud one?"

He was answered: "No, he won't. He looks serious, and he has a straight nose."

There were many, and every time we would pick up our shaven heads to take a look.

"I'm telling you, he's going to start yelling because he has a pointy nose," Yeriga insisted.

And if the soldier did in fact yell, then everyone would laugh loudly that their prediction came true. It became customary for us to see the dying. Everyone was much more interested when we were read the dinner menu.

Here as in Maidan, we heard explosions. The enemy was firing at the only escape route we had.

Yeriga concluded: "You don't believe me, but I am telling you again, a little more and the Germans are going to attack, and we will have to retreat. That's why they are shooting only up this road. We don't have a different way out. The enemy is very careful and precise. Good-bye, Zina, your end has come. You will never get out of here!"

"Stop scaring me, I will leave and go back to school," I said.

"You are already knowledgeable, and what you experienced here, no account in any book will be the same. No one could write that kind of book, because the book will be wet from tears, and all the ink will be smudged, and no one will be able to read anything. Now I know everything myself," Yeriga explained.

)))

Sasha came from the trenches and told us the news. He had been elected a secretary of the regimental committee. He had a new bow on his coat. The ends of the bow reached his waist. Yeriga came up to him and started twisting the ends of his bow, and Sasha moved away from him, warning: "Don't make it dirty, can't you see it's brand-new?"

"Don't act too important, my hands are just washed, nothing will happen to your bow," Yeriga answered.

"I have an assignment for you, Zina. Come here," said Sasha. "This is big. Listen, you have to tell everyone, all your friends, throw down your arms, leave your positions, leave the trenches, and that's it. Nothing more for now. But you have to do this."

"Okay, I will say that," I answered.

"I'm going, why are you laughing?" Sasha questioned.

"No reason, just laughing. You became very important," I said.

"I am a needed person, Zina. I am not showing off, but I am really busy now. My face has to show it," Sasha replied.

That same day I fulfilled Sasha's assignment. Walking from cot to cot of the patients getting well, I would lean over and whisper in their ear: "Don't go back to your positions. Everyone should go home, and that's all."

Some of them stared at me, not comprehending what I was saying. Others just laughed and said: "As if we haven't heard this before. We know ourselves, we have to go. You should go outside and yell to everyone, run home! Or have a meeting and say it openly. Oh, Zina, Zina!"

I lay down on my cot and was disappointed. I thought that Sasha gave me a really big assignment, and they just laughed at me.

"Guys, look! There is a meeting, and so many people gathering! Let's go!"

)))

There was a big crowd; noise, screams. Captain Krapivansky stood on a pile of bricks. He was about to speak, but was interrupted by a heavyset colonel who came from our brigade headquarters who said: "Soldiers, loyal to Russia! You know about the pogrom in Kalush, you see yourselves what the revolution has led to.[6] You see yourselves how there needs to be more discipline. Give power back to the officers! In the worst case outcome the enemy will destroy us, and nobody will be able to go back home."

"We don't want to hear this! We don't want to! Krapivansky, say your speech!" yelled the soldiers.

Krapivansky, worried and gesturing, spoke to the surrounding soldiers: "Comrades! You of course have seen all the drunken soldiers.

I saw soldiers riding horses, and they had bottles of wine where their guns should have been. The strike was organized on purpose. Those higher up purposely gave liquor to our soldiers before the attack. A drunken crowd robbed the villages, and Cossacks from the Savage Division were raping girls in Kalush. There was preparation for all this. The high command with Kerensky in charge set up a goal to provoke a revolution. Don't give in to provocations! The generals want everything back to the way it was. Don't listen to them, my friends!"

The captain finished speaking, and the soldiers cheered. The colonel quickly walked to his car, and hurrying off to his division, yelled back: "We will arrest you! Bolshevik! We will arrest you!"

"Zina, what did he call him?" Yeriga asked me.

"Bolshevik," I said.

"Do you know what that is—a Bolshevik?" Yeriga asked.

"No, do you?" I replied.

"I know everything," he said.

"So tell me," I said.

"A Bolshevik, Zina, supports the working class. You see, they are for destroying the privileged class, and they are against exploitation. I can give you an explanation because Sasha explained it to me, and I have a head on my shoulders. You understand? This is how it is now, you fight in the war and you go home. The Bolsheviks will give us land, and it will be ours. We need to secure it from our enemy. Maybe more blood will be shed, you see because . . ."

"Yeriga! Explain clearer!" I demanded.

"All right, I am going to give you an example, we have two groups and . . ."

"Listen, Yeriga, I will help you! So there are two groups, the upper class and the lower class," I interrupted.

"Right, right, this is how it is. It's a war between the two," he replied.

"Yeriga, I am not from the upper class, you made fun of me though and called me an intelligent one," I pointed out.

"Of course you're not of the upper class, you are somewhere in the middle. You should stick with us though, we will prevail, just stick with us," he advised.

CHAPTER 15

Zina's hospital is evacuated before an attack. There is a general retreat. Zina's regiment disbands, and she prepares to leave the army and return home.

We woke up at night from the loud and rapid gunfire.

"Didn't I tell you? Well, now you are finished. I told you, we are doomed!" Yeriga exclaimed.

"Stop panicking, we don't know anything yet," I answered.

Everything started moving now. Everyone was pulling up their trousers and putting on their robes. Some people were throwing their clothes out of their bags, others were stuffing their bags with their belongings. Dr. DeMorrey ran over and yelled to a nurse: "Saddle the horse! Get the wagons ready! Load the wounded!"

"Why only the wounded?" There were many questions thrown at the doctor.

Nayumich was really lost, and his big body moved clumsily around the corridor.

"I beg you, don't worry! Whoever can, get up and get dressed. Everyone else, wait for a command," Nayumich told the soldiers.

"Enough! We have had enough commands, we understand everything ourselves!" came the response.

The gunfire was reaching us.

"Yeriga, I am going to take you by the arm, and we will walk, all right, dearest?" I said.

"Now I am dearest. It's always like that, when someone needs you, you become their dearest. All right, give me your hand and don't fall behind. Oh, Zina! We need only to get to the road! Then we'll go to Maidan, Povelichie, and to Stanislau. The road is familiar. Look, the batteries are moving! Wait for me, I forgot my balalaika," he added hurriedly.

"Forget it! Hurry, let's run!" I shouted.

"Forget it! Forget it! Then why are you dragging your bag along? Throw it away too! She has silk undergarments there! Throw it away! Button your shirt. Why did you stick your cross out? It's not going to help. We're going to die anyway," Yeriga responded.

The sick cried and begged to be put in the wagon. They cursed their friends who walked away, crawling after them. We ran out onto the road. A battery galloped past us. We heard their wagon wheels rumble hard against the timber road. The cavalry, in *burkas*, galloped past us.[1] The gunfire from the village of Studzianka became more rapid.[2] We ran along the road where the artillery fire was focused. Behind us I saw hospital wagons and Nayumich and nurse Vaska. Behind them were the doctors on horses. The Austrians began shelling us, and the shells fell on the timber road right in front of us. We heard noise and then separate screams, "Oh, take me with you! Oh, take me, brothers!" yelled a wounded soldier.

"Stay to the left, there are woodpiles here," a voice advised.

"Those asses arrested Krapivansky at the division headquarters!" yelled the messenger who ran towards the village.

We ran and stopped for a second, the stampede of people knocked us off our feet. We heard an explosion and following it a terrible breakdown around us.

"They set fire to the ammunition supply in the forest. Look, Zina, it's burning! The Crimeans probably got ahead of us and blew up their ammunition. We're finished," Yeriga said.

I saw a big red flame in the direction of the villages of Maidan and Nova Huta.[3] There was another explosion. Yeriga jumped into a ditch and pulled me with him. I threw down my belongings. The second we got in there we were squashed by several others. Yeriga didn't let go of my hand and repeated only one phrase: "We're going to die!"

We barely got out of the ditch. On the road there were footsteps, squeals, cursing, indistinguishable commands from the officers, and the neighing of horses. The forest was torn to pieces, howling and roaring under the flames. Shells were exploding, falling amid crowds of soldiers. Pieces of shrapnel were hitting hard against the treetops. Another shot and the horror. I put my hands over my ears and wanted to curl into a little ball to be as small as possible. My insides were completely frozen. I heard my heart beat. My ears hurt from the neighing of the wild, terrorized horses. They were afraid of fire and resisted any urges to move. Their riders kicked them in their sides. The soldiers whipped them. They broke free, stood up on their hind legs, and with a leap they ripped their reins and just ran aimlessly. Then I ran, and when a shell exploded, and I saw it wasn't near me, I breathed again. There were horrendous noises of explosions coming from the forest, and the echo wouldn't die down.

Sunrise; we were in the forest. The burning smell standing in the air made it hard to breathe. There was a fire ahead of us. A cavalryman rode past us and yelled: "Stop! The enemy's cavalry is to the left of us! Save yourselves!"

Soldiers panicked; the artillerymen cut their horses out of their harness, beat them with their sword scabbards, threw their guns away, and ran. Again someone yelled: "Save yourself! The cavalry!"

We ran forward with all our effort. Yeriga was dragging me. I slowed down, and my cross got stuck on a bush. Yeriga pulled me by the hand. I pulled on the ribbon, but it wouldn't come loose. I had to pull it off quickly. The sound of a shell was nearby. I let go of his hand and ran to the bush, and I found the cross. I quickly put it on and caught up with Yeriga. Someone pushed me. I fell to the ground, and looking up, I saw I couldn't catch up with Yeriga. I got so mad at the cross, I thought, it's all your fault I got held up.

I remembered Yeriga's words, leave it, it won't help you anyway, and either way we will get killed. I threw it down again, but this time a shell exploded right by me, and I felt it on my leg. I grabbed my leg, it didn't hurt. It was only a clump of dirt. I opened my fist and put on the cross again. In this moment of chaos and insanity I realized the only thing that could help me was my own two feet. I depended on their speed, and all I needed to do was run to a covering before everyone filled it up and hide from the explosions. The prayers I murmured when the shells were exploding nearby only distracted my concentration. My mother and nanny used to say, get on your knees, pray for a long time and pray well, God will help you. But in reality, if I stopped, then I would get trampled and die. I don't ever want to pray again. I had to run, and that was the only thing that would save me.

I saw the face of Dybelo, he was hitting his horse. It was afraid of the explosions and the burning trees. There was a loud explosion. He fell off the horse, and someone yelled: "Good, that's what he deserves!"

)))

The village of Uhryniv; here I saw Trofim.[4] He hopped about on one leg, leaning on his rifle. He had an officer's revolver tucked in his belt. His trousers were covered in blood, and he wore no hat or coat. He closely followed a cart overloaded with the wounded.

"Trofim, are you hurt?" I asked.

"I was hit a little by shrapnel. Zina, Zinochka, how am I going to go home now? Am I really going to stay here? What about Klavdyshka? What about Mashka and Vacya? And how will I go home without presents? I lost all my money! Oh God!" he lamented.

In half an hour we left the village. The cavalry was putting fields of wheat on fire. Cavalrymen with torches galloped through the village, accompanied by shouts of "Burn everything! Why did you stop?" There was a little hut at the edge of the village. A woman sat on the doorstep surrounded by children. She was on her knees and begged them not to leave her without a home.

"You don't have a husband, you unworthy bitch! Your Austrian husband went against us! Let her have it, guys!" shouted a cavalryman. The riders lashed the woman with a whip, and the children ran out into the blazing wheat field.

We went backward. We didn't leave the burning area we were in.

The road led to Tysmenytsia.[5] One of the artilleryman brought news that the Germans had already taken Tarnopol.[6] There were rumors of the capture of Volochysk.[7] News spread that we were being encircled. Nobody stopped to think; they just walked. During the day we walked through all the huts in search of food. At night we searched for the road. And shortly the movement of troops was identifiable by the conflagrations, and the sky was enveloped by a scarlet horseshoe.

The wheat fields were burning. I looked into the smoke and remembered yesterday. A girl ran through the burning fields, away from the cavalry. They got to her, hopped off their horses, raped her, and pulling up their trousers and fixing their coats, they yelled to the others to hurry up. There was smoke in the blue sky and blood on her blouse.

〉〉〉

Near the road, some fellow was leading his cow along with her calf. The calf, spooked by the oncoming wagon, jumped over a ditch. I heard a crack. They ran over the calf's head. The cow, stretching its neck, mooed loudly. The fellow threw down his straw hat and ran in the direction of the village.

The mobile hospital went by.

"Zina, Zina, look!" It was Trofim stretching his legs out, smiling, yelling, and waving to me.

"Trofim! Hello! They took you with them?" I yelled.

"Hello and good-bye, Zina! Now I am going to Russia, to Lipki! Farewell!"

The wheels began turning on the dusty road. Trofim rode away. I looked in his direction for a long, long time.

〉〉〉

We walked five versts. The regiment, of which less than forty people were left, didn't get held up for long. The carriages passed us. Plakhov and Balme sat in one of them. Some of the soldiers, seeing Plakhov, got out of line, ran up to the horses and pulled on their reins, making them stop. They shouted:

"Let's settle old accounts!"

"We'll show you!"

"We'll ride you around!"

Somebody whistled, and then there was an even louder whistle. In a few seconds the soldiers surrounded the colonel.

"Get him, guys!" yelled one of the Stavropolsky Regiment soldiers.

"Start with his stomach!" yelled another.

Balme stood there gripping his sword.

"Drag him by the beard!" yelled a soldier.

Plakhov reached for his revolver, but the soldiers immediately got hold of his hands and feet and pulled him to the bushes. His eyes filled up with blood, and he was foaming at the mouth. His face was scary. The colonel tried to fight them off with his legs.

"Stab him!" shouted a soldier.

He let out a wild, beastly scream. It echoed as if another beast answered his cry. Then there was a rise of laughter: "He's done! We killed him!"

You couldn't see him. The soldiers all around blocked his corpse. I saw Yeriga among their heads. The soldiers straightened out and moved away. I saw Yeriga clapping his hands, whistling, dancing on Plakhov's stomach.

Pulling off Balme's boots, they pushed him and yelled, "Go away!"

He went in the direction of the forest.

The soldiers, lining up again, walked on.

)))

A bloody pig ran from the village of Ybayuvka in our direction. The animal made wild, squealing noises. A bunch of artillerymen ran after it with knives.

"Catch her! Get her!" they yelled.

The pig ran towards the forest, and it wouldn't stop squealing. But soon the chase was over. The artillerymen caught the pig. Six soldiers with bloody army coats and rolled-up sleeves began to cut out the pig's fat. Their dull knives brought great agony and torture to the animal. It couldn't even squeal anymore, it just shook its head violently and grinding its teeth, tried to get out of their hold. After the soldiers cut out a great big piece from the pig, they let the animal go. The disfigured pig ran away.

)))

We were at the village of Lisna Slobidka.[8] Somewhere in the distance there were gunshots heard. There were no people in the streets. The huts were ruined. There were small trenches on the edge of the village.

I sat at the same well as yesterday. I slept all day and all night in a small trench. The regiment was far away. Yeriga probably searched for me. I had hoped that maybe I would catch some wagon passing by and go with them. Sections of the Seventh Division passed by, but their wagons were full of wounded soldiers, and there was no sense in even trying to get in one. I didn't care what happened to me, but the thought of marching was so frightening now. My legs wouldn't obey. I couldn't take it anymore. I decided not to leave the village. Gunfire, but it was far away. I still have to get up, I could be captured. I willed myself to get up, but fell back on the hard ground. Did it matter what I slept on? I had a soft bed at home. For a second I imagined my mother by my clean, soft bed, but I forced myself to get up. I forced myself to walk onto the road. I picked up a cap from the ground and climbed up a tall tree. A wagon passed by, then a small group of infantry, followed by a group of cavalry. It was obviously our rear guard. This must have been the last of our division. The village was empty. Now we could await the Austrians. The bright sunset lit up the horizon.

"No, you don't get it, you have to leave!" I said out loud to myself and continued to sit in the tree. I felt like I turned into a bubble and was empty inside. I would pop any minute, and there would be nothing left of me.

I looked at the road. In the distance I saw a line of soldiers in gray-blue coats, and all of a sudden I felt very uneasy. They walked into the sunset to the west of the forest. There was a little cloud of dust on the road and a dark spot. It became bigger and bigger. Nearing, it became clearer and clearer. I thought it was a rider. I opened my eyes wider as if that would help me see better. After a few minutes I clearly saw a person in a dark shirt. He waved his hand above the horse. He was nearing, closer and closer. He looked like he was on his way to the well where I slept. Circling it, he rode back to the village.

To the left there seemed to be a group of riders in gray-blue coats. The firing ceased. It was the Austrians; now what?

My heart was racing as I climbed down the tree. I ran out into the road. The rider lifted himself in his saddle, and I saw the familiar, thin waist of Yeriga. The blood rushed to my head. I wanted to yell to him, but I couldn't. I had such an overwhelming feeling. I saw my friend. He reached his hands to me, and I jumped up onto the back of the horse. We galloped on in silence through the village, along the road over a hill. I looked at the horizon, and this whole war seemed to me like an ugly, scary mask of death.

As in a kaleidoscope, my first days in the war twirled in my head. My reasons for coming here and leaving home seemed stupid and funny now. And now, only now, did I understand why I left home the second time.

I left to go to the people. I came to a new family, and the hurt I felt at being left alone was slowly disappearing because of this horseback rider.

We stopped to rest. I looked at Yeriga. His cheeks were bright. His little eyes were swollen from the wind and pollen.

"Yeriga! You're a real friend!" I squeezed his hand. He smiled, showing his white teeth.

"What did you think? A friend is not just a title, a friend is a friend," he said, wiping his face. "We looked for you. I thought you got picked up by a Seventh Division cart, but the guys said that they thought they saw you by a house near the road. Comrade Ivanov went to the Krimsky Regiment to hold a meeting, and I went to get you."

"Yeriga, where is the regiment? Where is Sasha?" I asked.

He answered: "We will catch up to the division, but Sasha, oh, Zina, they killed him! They killed him at one of those meetings. Don't think he forgot about you. He wanted to go with us to look for you. He was asking the Seventh Division about you. But he couldn't, duty called and he had to go to that meeting."

"Yeriga!" I yelled tearfully.

"Hey there, don't cry, Zina! Sasha told me you are going to go to school to become a doctor. I know everything, he told me about it all. So, stick with your word. Come visit me in the village. Don't cry, I know it's hard for you because you loved him. Look at this! You completely soaked my hand with your tears! Here, take the handkerchief. It's all right, it will pass. You are young, everything will be all right. You see, they killed him on the job; now you get started on yours. You will be successful. You have a lot of energy. Come visit us." he said.

"All right, I'll come visit," I answered.

APPENDIX

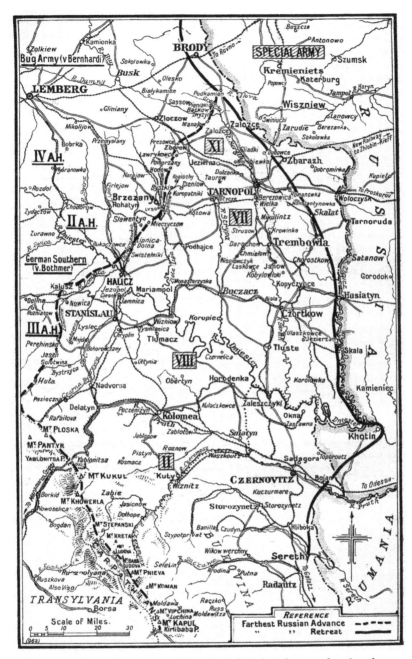

Fig. 1. Map of Russian army positions in Galicia in July 1917 showing the area of operations of Zina's army unit. *The Times History of the War*, vol. 14 (London: "The Times," Printing House Square, 1918), 14.

Fig. 2. Map depicting the towns of Studinka, Vistova, Maidan, Nova Huta, and Uhryniv in relation to Stanislau (Ivano-Frankivsk).

NOTES

INTRODUCTION

1. Deborah Sampson's biography has been widely written about in articles and books since the eighteenth century. One of the earliest accounts of her life is Herman Mann, *The Female Review, or Memoirs of an American Young Lady* (Dedham MA: Nathaniel and Benjamin Heaton, Printers, 1797).
2. "Fighting Value of the Jew," *The Literary Digest*, January 30, 1897, 407–8.
3. "A Female Soldier and Her Experiences—Cupid in the Leading-Strings of Mars," *Massachusetts Spy* (Worcester MA), June 3, 1862, 3.
4. Vincent Y. C. Shih, *The Taiping Ideology: Its Sources, Interpretations, and Influences* (Seattle: University of Washington Press, 1967): 62–65; "Paris," *Memphis Daily Appeal*, May 16, 1871: 1; "The Chinaman's Better Half," *New York Tribune*, January 21, 1912, 4.
5. "Russian Women Dash into Ranks When Troops Fall During Battle; Wounded Girls Fill One Hospital," *Washington Post*, September 12, 1915, Section 2, 5; Byron Lomax, "Many Women Are Among Armies in Conflict," *San Francisco Chronicle*, February 21, 1915, 54. Maria Botchkareva, a decorated woman soldier, helped establish and became the commander of the Russian Women's Battalion of Death under the auspices of Alexander Kerensky's revolutionary provisional government in the summer of 1917. The short-lived Women's Battalion of Death proved its worth as a combat unit in a single engagement on the eastern front and provided the impetus for the formation of other women's combat units. Prior to the overthrow of Kerensky's government in November 1917 by the Bolsheviks, the Russian army had begun mobilizing about 10,000 women for additional all-women combat units. These new women's units, however, were quickly disbanded by the Bolshevik government, which subsequently raised its own all-female combat units.
6. "Russian Women in Cossack Ranks," *San Francisco Chronicle*, November 4, 1914, 13.

7. "Russian Women Dash into Ranks," *Washington Post*, September 12, 1915, Section 2, 5; "Young Girls Fighting on the Russian Front," *The New York Times Current History—The European War*, Vol. 7, April–June 1916, (New York: New York Times Company, 1917), 365–67.

8. It was not until 2001 that a second account of a female soldier, the English language memoirs of Maria Botchkareva, *My Life as a Peasant, Soldier and Exile* (1918), was translated and published in Russia. Botchkareva's memoir was not published in Russia during the Soviet era because she was considered a counter-revolutionary by the Soviet government.

9. Kazan was the capital of Tatarstan.

10. The information is taken from an article about Osip Mandelstam by Paval M. Nerler on the Russian internet webpage Zhurnal'nyi zal (Magazine room): http://magazines.russ.ru/novyi_mi/2016/2/v-moskve-noyabr-1930 -maj-1934.html, accessed January 5, 2018.

11. Clarence Brown, *Mandelstam* (New York: Cambridge University Press, 1978), 127.

12. Russian internet webpage.

13. "Women's Death Battalion Story Told in Book," *Seattle Daily Times*, April 30, 1930, 17. The article mistakenly credited Tatiana Dubinskaya as being a member of the Russian Women's Battalion of Death, organized in 1917, which she was not.

CHAPTER 1

1. Kazatin was about 1,850 kilometers southwest of Kazan, in the western Ukraine.

2. Brody was about three hundred kilometers west of Kazatin. It was a strategic rail center in Austro-Hungarian eastern Galicia that bordered the Russian Empire and was about eight kilometers west of the Russian frontier. Zina appears to have run away from home and joined the army no earlier than the spring of 1916, but it is unlikely she could have been at Brody during this period since the Austrians occupied the town from September 2, 1915, to July 28, 1916.

CHAPTER 2

1. Zinaedische was a nickname given to Zina by her father.

2. Gai was about three kilometers southeast of Brody.

3. A *verst* is approximately one kilometer.

4. The Russian army captured the Austrian fortress at Przemyśl, in Galicia, in March 1915.

5. Zastavki was about 145 kilometers southwest of Brody.

6. Russian soldiers wore *portyanki*, rectangular pieces of cloth worn wrapped around the feet.

7. Communications trenches were constructed at an angle to a defensive trench and often used to transport men and supplies to the front line.
8. Poltava Gubernia was a Ukrainian administrative-territorial unit of the Russian empire that bordered on Chernigov and Kursk Gubernia in the north, on Kharkov Gubernia in the east, on Ekaterinoslav and Kherson Gubernia in the south, and on Kiev Gubernia in the west.
9. The St. Vladimir Order had four degrees and was awarded for continuous civil and military service.
10. A *bashlik* was a hooded Cossack headdress.

CHAPTER 3

1. Shrapnel was an antipersonnel artillery munition composed of small lead ball projectiles that were intended to explode in an air burst over a target.

CHAPTER 4

1. Mikhalka was about 120 kilometers southeast of Brody.
2. Zalischyky, captured by Russia on June 14, 1916, was located about 120 kilometers south of Tarnopol on the Dniester River. Okna, captured by Russia on June 10, 1916, was located about sixty-five kilometers southeast of Zalischyky on the Yahorlyk River, a branch of the Dniester River.
3. The Tekintsi were a Turkman Muslim tribe.
4. *Krones* were Austrian money.

CHAPTER 5

1. Russian officers were armed with pistols and swords and did not normally carry rifles.
2. The Days of the Holy Trinity are also known as the Pentecost in the Eastern Orthodox Church and include the fifty days after Easter.

CHAPTER 6

1. The Russian army normally carried rifles with fixed bayonets.
2. *Uhlans* were lancers.

CHAPTER 7

1. *Moskaliki* is a Ukrainian term meaning "Russians."
2. Nikitovka was a village in the easternmost region of Ukraine, part of the Luhansk Oblast (Province).
3. Kolpin was a Polish village about ten kilometers west of Brody and about two hundred kilometers east of Warsaw.
4. *Guten Tag*, literally "good day," means "hello" in German.
5. "My friend, would you like to be a prisoner of war?"
6. "I am grateful to you."
7. "Female, female!"

CHAPTER 8

1. Koropets was a Ukrainian village on the Dniester River located about ninety kilometers southwest of Tarnopol. The Russian army conducted operations in the area in mid-August 1916.
2. Guta Penyatska was a Ukrainian village about fifty kilometers northwest of Tarnopol.
3. The Russo-Turkish War (1877–78).

CHAPTER 9

1. Rokitno was about 185 kilometers southeast of Guta Penyatska and about ten kilometers west of Dolzhok.
2. Preference is a complex Russian card game that is sometimes called *pul'ka*.
3. Dolzhok was about 145 kilometers southeast of Tarnopol.

CHAPTER 10

1. The St. George Cross was the highest military award available to Russian soldiers and had four classes or degrees.

CHAPTER 11

1. Zhmerynka was about 135 kilometers southeast of Rokitno in the central Ukraine.
2. Only general officers wore red-lined coats.
3. Bryansk was about 1,200 kilometers southwest of Kazan.
4. Rasputin was a Russian peasant, mystical faith healer, and private adviser to the Romanovs, who was murdered on December 30, 1916, in St. Petersburg.

CHAPTER 12

1. Tarnopol was about 945 kilometers southwest of Bryansk.
2. Buchach was about seventy kilometers southwest of Tarnopol.
3. Monastorzyska was about fifteen kilometers west of Buchach.
4. Medieval student's anthem, in Latin.
5. Mezo Laborez was about sixty-five kilometers west of Przemyśl.

CHAPTER 13

1. Czar Nicholas II abdicated as the ruler of Russia on March 2 (Julian calendar)/March 15, (Gregorian calendar) 1917.
2. *Tovarisch* means "comrade."
3. "Like an hourglass!"
4. "Are you looking for someone?"
5. "Oh! Kohgler! He went your way, he was wounded last night and evacuated to the rear of the army."
6. Stanislau (currently named Ivano-Frankivsk) was about 70 kilometers southwest of Buchach.

7. Alexander F. Kerensky, Minister of Justice, in the Russian Provisional Government that replaced the Romanov dynasty, assumed the additional responsibility of Minister of War in May 1917.

8. The March 1917 revolution ushered in regimental soldiers' committees throughout the Russian army. All military orders had to be submitted to these committees, often composed of activist soldiers with their own agendas, and approved by them before being issued to the troops. Their ability to veto the recommendations of their commanders greatly interfered with the conduct of military operations.

9. The "Savage Division" was an elite Cossack cavalry division.

10. General Alexei Brusilov was appointed Commander-in-Chief of the Russian Army in May 1917.

11. Albert Thomas was a French Socialist and the first Minister of Armament for the French Third Republic during World War I.

12. *The Truth about the Trenches* was a revolutionary newspaper.

CHAPTER 14

1. Yamnytsya was about ten kilometers north of Stanislau.

2. The skull and crossbones insignia were worn by special army units, composed largely of loyal officers, which were sworn to fight to the death in continuing the war. Such a unit was known as a "Battalion of Death."

3. Pidpechery was about eight kilometers southeast of Yamnytsya.

4. Maidan was about ten kilometers northwest of Yamnytsya.

5. Vistova was about twenty-two kilometers northeast of Pidpechery and about eight kilometers northwest of Maidan.

6. Kalush was about twelve kilometers northeast of Vistova.

CHAPTER 15

1. A *burka* was a customary cloak of various peoples from the Caucasus.

2. Studzianka (present day Studinka) was one kilometer northwest of Vistova.

3. Nova Huta was four kilometers southeast of Maidan.

4. Uhryniv was about twelve kilometers southeast of Maidan.

5. Tysmenytsia was about 115 kilometers southwest of Tarnopol.

6. The Germans captured Tarnopol between July 22 and July 23, 1917. See "Teuton Sweep Threatens to Shatter Russian Armies," *New York Tribune*, July 24, 1917, 2.

7. Volochysk was about forty-five kilometers east of Tarnopol.

8. Lisna Slobidka was about fifty kilometers southeast of Stanislau.

INDEX

CPSIA information can be obtained
at www.ICGtesting.com
Printed in the USA
LVHW111613180120
644022LV00008B/513